Rome Tales

Rome Tales

Stories selected
and translated by

Hugh Shankland

Edited by

Helen Constantine

OXFORD
UNIVERSITY PRESS

OXFORD
UNIVERSITY PRESS

Great Clarendon Street, Oxford OX2 6DP

Oxford University Press is a department of the University of Oxford.
It furthers the University's objective of excellence in research, scholarship,
and education by publishing worldwide in

Oxford New York

Auckland Cape Town Dar es Salaam Hong Kong Karachi
Kuala Lumpur Madrid Melbourne Mexico City Nairobi
New Delhi Shanghai Taipei Toronto

With offices in

Argentina Austria Brazil Chile Czech Republic France Greece
Guatemala Hungary Italy Japan Poland Portugal Singapore
South Korea Switzerland Thailand Turkey Ukraine Vietnam

Oxford is a registered trade mark of Oxford University Press
in the UK and in certain other countries

Published in the United States
by Oxford University Press Inc., New York

© General introduction Helen Constantine 2011
Introduction, selection, notes, translation Hugh Shankland 2011

The moral rights of the authors have been asserted
Database right Oxford University Press (maker)

First published 2011

British Library Cataloguing in Publication Data

Data available

Library of Congress Cataloging in Publication Data

Library of Congress Control Number: 2009924591

Typeset by SPI Publisher Services, Pondicherry, India
Printed in Great Britain
on acid-free paper by
Clays Ltd., St Ives plc

ISBN 978–0–19–957246–5

1 3 5 7 9 10 8 6 4 2

Contents

General Introduction   1

Introduction   5

Abraham the Jew
Giovanni Boccaccio   13

Release
Pier Paolo Pasolini   21

The New Thérèse
Giacomo Casanova   35

The Shirt on the Wall
Erri De Luca   43

Cola di Rienzo
Anonymous Roman   51

Freedom
Goffredo Parise   77

Blue Car
Melania Mazzucco   87

Via Veneto Notes
Ennio Flaiano   97

Lorette Ellerup
Francesco Mandica   121

Two Days to Christmas
Elisabetta Rasy   133

Isabella De Luna
Matteo Bandello   147

The Rubber Twins
Vincenzo Cerami   155

The Beautiful Hand
Giorgio Vigolo   163

The Girl with the Braid
Dacia Maraini   179

16 October 1943
Giacomo Debenedetti   191

Samia
Sandro Onofri   215

Exmatriates
Igiaba Scego   223

Romulus and Remus
Alberto Moravia   247

The Small Hours
Corrado Alvaro   259

The Sound of Woodworm
Giosuè Calaciura   269

Notes on the Authors   276

Further Reading and Viewing   281

Publisher's Acknowledgements   285

Map of Rome   287

Picture Credits

General Introduction

Rome Tales, the fourth in the series of City Tales, is a collection of twenty stories, all set in Rome. Although they span seven hundred years of writing by Italians, they are not arranged chronologically. Instead old and new appear side by side, apparently without order until the adventure of reading discloses subtle sequences and connections. This freer approach intentionally mirrors Rome's unpredictability, the many possibilities for surprise that await a visitor to this extraordinary city where—like an ice cream van parked in front of the Colosseum—great fragments of the past pervade the immediate present of a twenty-first-century metropolis. Of course, it is not historical monuments that make a city—even if that city is Rome—but the living continuum of its inhabitants, and in these tales their separate stories seem to intertwine, often in the common struggle to make sense of their lives within what Ennio Flaiano in the eighth tale represents as two Romes, the brash and hectic, and the more intimate and personal.

On the day-to-day level, more than any other great city Rome is caught between two more or less incompatible contending realities: the vitality of a modern capital city in constant expansion, and the inertia of an ancient city centre that is one of the wonders of the world, a repository of incalculable numbers of treasures of artistic, archaeological, religious, and historical significance that make it one of the most popular tourist destinations in Europe. The importance to Western civilization of Rome, the Republic, and the Roman Empire needs no reiterating. The role of Rome in the growth and consolidation of Christianity made the city again a great centre of authority in the medieval period. Due to the immense wealth and patronage of the papacy, the city became the acknowledged centre of European artistic and cultural life during the Renaissance and Baroque ages. Though Rome then slumbered on in increasing political irrelevance, beautiful and neglected, for northern Europeans it remained the chief destination of the Grand Tour until at least the Napoleonic Wars. Its role from 1870 as capital city of a newly unified Italy suddenly thrust it into the modern age. Mussolini, with his ambitions to be a new Caesar, exploited the powerful myth of Rome in the Italian historical consciousness, tearing down many picturesque old neighbourhoods in the inner city to make way for grand settings for martial parades, or great displays of public oratory in Piazza Venezia within sight of the ancient Forum. The Pope, sovereign ruler of the city for some fourteen hundred years, was relegated to the tiny independent enclave of Vatican City.

Many readers of the opening story by Boccaccio may be surprised, even shocked, to discover that the Pope's authority, much disputed in our secular, sceptical age, was already under attack even within Italy as long ago as the mid-fourteenth century. This witty tale of the conversion to Christianity of 'Abraham the Jew' despite the spectacle of the moral degradation of the papal court in Rome, 'a hotbed of works of the devil', plunges the reader straight into a confrontation with Rome as myth and reality. The concluding story, a fantasy about the loneliness of the ageing Polish Pope at the mercy of his minders, rounds off the volume with perfect symmetry.

The anthology is extremely varied in subject matter, style, and tone: Vigolo's intriguing investigations into the 'mysterious impersonal memory' of ancient houses in the historic centre in his story about the beautiful hands of Costanza; Melania Mazzucco's 'Blue Car' about a school trip to Rome; Igiaba Scego's 'Exmatriates' with its humorous and yet 'dead serious' dissection of the dilemma of national identity felt by longer term immigrants in Rome; Cerami's bizarre tale of the 'Rubber Twins'; Moravia's 'Romulus and Remus' with its portrait of urban poverty;

Debenedetti's deeply moving, sparely-written account of the Nazi round-up of the Jews of the Ghetto. Each writer has his or her special voice: wry, reflective, questioning, poetic.

The coincidence that ROMA/AMOR is a palindrome was made much of by Goethe in his 'Roman Elegies'. Rome is a city that inspires love in those who visit as well as those who live there, and we hope this anthology, a testament to the Italian writers' and the English translator's love of Rome, will do the same.

As in other volumes in this series of City Tales, each tale is illustrated by a black and white photo which provides a particular reflection or emblem of that story. Notes on the Authors will be found at the back of the book, along with suggestions for Further Reading and Viewing, and a Map of Rome to help readers locate some of the more important sites which feature in the texts.

Helen Constantine

Introduction

In selecting and arranging this score of stories of Rome my aim has been to present them in such a way that readers have the pleasure of making their own discoveries and connections, just as happens when one sets out—in good company—to explore a new city. So I shall not say too much about them.

Boccaccio's great tale of 'Abraham the Jew', written around 1350, stands here as a prologue and portal to many more narratives of Rome since the Parisian Jew's discovery of the devastating truth about the capital of Christendom and the startling conclusion he draws memorably dramatize the Eternal City's central conundrum and fascination, its endlessly contradictory and metamorphic nature, and its no less profound underlying continuity. The common factor in the next three stories (2, 3, 4) is that they too concern the anticipation and the experience of entering the city, albeit in different times and in very different moods. The love story 'The Shirt on the Wall' (4), with its heady atmosphere of grass-roots revolt and 'war' in the streets of Rome during the idealistic student uprising of the late sixties which was to degenerate into the extremes of urban terror and state repression in the seventies, is immediately followed by a graphic account of class warfare and demagoguery in the Middle Ages, just one of many particularly violent episodes in the city's age-old power struggle between patricians and plebeians: Cola di Rienzo's people's revolution vividly recalled by a fourteenth-century eyewitness, one of the masterpieces of early Italian literature (5). From very different perspectives, stories 6 and 7 offer two takes on Rome as the centre of political power in our own day.

For all their subjectivity, Ennio Flaiano's wry 'Via Veneto Notes' (8) is a piece of historical writing because of its keen sense of Rome changing irrevocably—'bigger, nastier, richer'—during the very years in which he and Federico Fellini were devising *La dolce vita*. Although like almost every other great city on the planet Rome has become much more problematic than the one which Flaiano dissected in 1958–62, visitors will still recognize many features of his 'different city' fifty years on. His sardonic reflections on sex and the city are followed here by six contrasting stories of women (9–14), two of whom lived centuries ago.

Dacia Maraini's poignant tale of a young country girl's struggle for life in the perplexing city (14) seemed to me to form an appropriate bridge between this section and three tales of settlers in Rome, beginning with Giacomo Debenedetti's account of the SS round-up in 1943 of one thousand Jews still living on the site of the ancient ghetto (15). I chose this noble testimony not only for its great human and literary qualities but also to bring home to the reader yet again—as in the case of Cola di Rienzo—the long and painful history of post-classical Rome and its long-suffering inhabitants.

There has been a Jewish colony in Rome from at least the second century BC. Although under the medieval popes Jews had to wear distinctive clothing when outside their settlements in the districts of Regola, Ripa, and Sant'Angelo, they still operated freely within the surrounding Christian society and some held positions at the papal court as physicians and administrators. The loss of all their rights as citizens except as taxpayers and their confinement to the narrow streets around Piazza Giudia, the area of densest settlement, did not occur until the mid-sixteenth century during the most repressive phase of the Counter-Reformation. Shamefully, no pope thought to tear down the gates to the ghetto until this was done for them by Napoleon and again by the conquering Italian state in 1870.

Although I have included no tales from classical times, many different epochs in the city's changing history are recalled. There is the lawless Rome abandoned by the papacy and terrorized by feuding baronial families in Cola di Rienzo's time. There is the splendour and decadence of Renaissance Rome, 'our universal mother', eulogized by Bandello in his wonderful tale of the spirited courtesan Isabella De Luna (11). There is the stifling atmosphere of Counter-Reformation Rome in Giorgio Vigolo's ghost story, 'The Beautiful Hand' (13). There are the society salons and worldly clerics and foreign artists encountered in the Casanova snapshot of mid-eighteenth-century Rome (3).

Closer to our own times, there is the depressed Rome of the Second World War and the immediate post-war years in Debenedetti and Moravia's stories (15, 18), and in Pasolini's somehow lyrical description of the scarred landscape and slum suburbs of 'shanties and grim towers' in the early 1950s (2). Then there is Flaiano's hedonistic Rome during the boom years of Italy's 'economic miracle' and a rather less impressive 'cultural miracle' against which he sketches the unforgettable figure of the ageing poet Cardarelli. (8).

As in the cases of Boccaccio's Abraham or the 'old elephant' poet who so fascinated Flaiano, many of these stories concern outsiders—migrants, visitors, tourists: the penniless young southern Italian migrant for whom 'Rome is first of all the railway station' (4), the timid

country 'girl with the braid' (14), the unscrupulous operator Casanova (3), the visiting school party (7), the apparently 'completely normal couple' of Danish tourists
(9), the blissfully innocent or ignorant young American
painter in the Villa Borghese (6), and of course the supreme insider-outsider, Pope John Paul II (20). Two
memorably told contrasting stories which I have placed
immediately after the account of the fate of the Jews in
1943 concern the lives of just a few of the many foreign
migrants in the city in our own time (16, 17). Finally,
there is Corrado Alvaro's profoundly subtle tale of the
chance encounter between three English tourists and a
group of long-time friends who discover that the city
they thought they knew so well, too well, is still a potential
theatre for human redemption (19). Incidentally, it is
worth taking a practical cue from what Alvaro says
about 'nocturnal Rome': the most magical thing one can
ever do in this wonderful city is wander through it during
'the small hours', and then when the first few bars begin to
open for those who have to be at work by six or seven join
them in the warm for a strong coffee.

In this story, and in two or three others in the collection, the narrator seems to be groping towards some
(impossible?) definition of Rome, or rather towards
what Rome, at the deepest level, might mean for those
who live there. Despite his disgust at all he sees, even

Boccaccio's wise Jew comes to derive spiritual meaning and the profoundest comfort for his soul from meditating on the seven deadly sins as practised in the Holy City. The contemporary visitor, too, though bewildered and frustrated and even disillusioned by much that he sees in this turbulent modern metropolis which is after all only one more layer on top of a ten-metre-thick subsoil of human history reaching back more than two and a half millennia, will almost certainly end up 'converted'. Just ask Lorette Ellerup! In Rome there are simply so many riches to discover for oneself, and warm to, as these stories will show.

Hugh Shankland

Abraham the Jew

Giovanni Boccaccio

I have been told, fair ladies, that in Paris dwelt a great merchant and most estimable man whose name was Jeanot de Chevigny, very dependable and honest and a leading light in the drapery trade, the close friend of a very rich Jew named Abraham, himself a supremely honest and dependable merchant. Seeing his great qualities, Jeanot came sorely to regret that the soul of such an admirable and wise and good man should go to perdition because he was an unbeliever. So in the most friendly fashion he began to entreat him to renounce the error of the Jewish faith and accept the truth of Christianity which, as he could see for himself, being most holy and good was prospering and growing all the time; whereas it was equally evident that his own was declining and almost dwindling to nothing. The Jew answered that he acknowledged none but the Jewish faith holy and good and that he was born into it, and there he intended to live and die, nor would anything ever induce him to renounce it. Undeterred, some days later Jeanot returned to the subject, expounding in the rough and ready way of most merchants for what reasons our faith was better than that of the Jews. And the Jew, for all that he was a great master in the Jewish religion, moved by his great friendship for Jeanot or perhaps persuaded by words which the Holy Ghost set on the untutored man's tongue, began to be powerfully taken with Jeanot's arguments; even so, remaining resolute in his belief, he would not let himself be converted.

The more he persisted in his obduracy the more Jeanot renewed his entreaties, and worn down by such relentless insistence the Jew finally said: 'Listen, Jeanot, you want me to become a Christian, and I am of a mind to do so; on one condition however, that I first go to Rome and there see for myself this man whom you say is the Vicar of God on earth and observe his life and his conduct, and the same with his brothers the cardinals. And if to me they appear such that both through your words and their example I can be convinced that your faith is better than mine, as you have striven to prove, I shall do as I promised; if not, I shall remain the Jew I am.'

When Jeanot heard this he was most perturbed, inwardly thinking: 'All the effort I thought I had put to such good purpose is wasted, and just when I was sure I had converted the man, since if he goes to the court of Rome and sees the iniquitous and foul life of the clergy, far from a Jew becoming Christian, had he already become Christian he would assuredly go back to being a Jew.' And turning to Abraham he said: 'Great heavens, my friend, why do you want to go to the trouble and enormous expense of going all the way from here to Rome, not to mention that for such a rich man as yourself there are infinite perils both on land and sea? Do you not suppose someone can be found here to baptize you? And if it be you still have some doubts concerning the faith I have expounded, where better than here will you find greater masters and wiser men to instruct you in whatever else you wish to know or ask about it? Therefore, in my view, this journey you propose is quite unnecessary. Believe me, the prelates there are just like any you have seen or could see here, and even better for being so much nearer the supreme Pastor himself. And so I would advise you to put off this exertion until such time as you may need to seek an indulgence, when all being well I could keep you company.'

To which the Jew replied: 'I believe everything is just as you say, Jeanot, but the long and the short of it is if you wish me to do what you have so much entreated, I am quite set on going, otherwise I shall never agree to it.'

Jeanot, seeing such resolution, said: 'And then God speed,' privately convinced he would never become a Christian once he had seen the court of Rome. Still, as it would not change matters, he said no more.

The Jew mounted his horse and as speedily as possible made his way to the court of Rome, where on arrival he was honourably welcomed by his fellow Jews. Settling down there, but without telling anyone what he had come for, he cautiously began to observe the behaviour of the Pope and the cardinals, and the other prelates and members of the court; and between what he saw for himself as a most perceptive man, and what other people told him, he found that in general from first to last all of them most scandalously sinned in lust, and not only in the natural way but the sodomitic, unconstrained by scruple or shame, to the extent that the power of whores and pretty boys to procure any great favour was almost beyond imagining. On top of that, they were all of them guzzlers and tipplers and drunkards, as was plain to see, and next to their lust like brute beasts more in thrall to their bellies than anything else. And as he went deeper into the matter he came to see they were all so miserly and greedy for money that human blood, and Christian at that, and even the most godly things of no matter what kind, from the offerings of the faithful to church benefices, they bought and sold for money, making a bigger business out of it and generating more middlemen than Paris possessed in the entire drapery trade or any other, renaming blatant simony 'procuration' and greed 'subsistence', as though God did not know let alone the meaning of words but the intentions of the blackest souls, and just like men can be gulled by the names of things. And all these things and many more unmentionable deeply disturbed the Jew, who was himself a sober and clean-living man, and deciding he had seen more than enough he resolved to return to Paris, and did forthwith. Hearing of his safe return, and not for one moment hoping he would ever become a Christian, Jeanot called on him, and both were overjoyed at seeing each other again. Finally, after letting him rest up a few days, Jeanot asked him about his impressions of the Holy Father and cardinals and other members of the papal court.

The Jew promptly replied: 'May God damn the lot of them—and I say this to you because, if my observations are worth anything, no holiness, no devotion, no good works, no moral example for life or anything else was to be found in so much as even one member of the clergy I saw there, while lust and avarice and greed, deceit and envy and pride, and similar and worse things, if worse can be, seemed to me to be in such favour with everyone there that I believe it to be more a hotbed of works of the devil than the godly. And from what I can judge, with every effort, and by every thought and means it seems your Pastor and consequently all the rest of them are doing all in their power to reduce the Christian religion to nothing and rid the world of it, when they should be its rock and foundation. Yet since I see that all they strive for fails to come about, and your religion is constantly expanding and becoming ever more lustrous and acclaimed, I have to conclude that the Holy Ghost itself must be its true rock and foundation, precisely because it is indeed more true and holy than any other. And this being so, where formerly I was unyielding in the face of all your exhortations and would not convert, I now freely declare that nothing can evermore prevent me from becoming a Christian. And so now let us go to a church, and there according to the rightful custom of your holy faith have me baptized.'

When Jeanot, who had expected the very opposite conclusion, heard him utter these words he was the happiest man who ever lived; and together they went to Notre-Dame in Paris where he asked the clergy there to baptize Abraham. Hearing this was indeed his wish, they at once did so; and Jeanot who was his sponsor at the sacred rite named him Jean, and then had certain very learned men fully instruct him in our faith which he very quickly mastered. And henceforth he lived a good and worthy man, and led a saintly life.

Release

Pier Paolo Pasolini

The great frontage of the Penitentiary jolted and slowly pulled back. Yellow and unadorned, its retreating bulk towered over the massive outer walls, also bare and yellow, behind which the other wing began to emerge like an enormous crate. The more the two buildings riddled with hundreds of windows diminished in size the starker they stood out against the milky sky and the ragged open countryside with not one tree as far as the eye could see.

To the right, the sentry-box loomed up empty and scabby as a urinal and rotating in the air dropped behind along with a glimpse of two *carabinieri* squatting in the dust with their rifles between their knees; then after breasting an abrupt incline, rotating too, came a noisy scene of ordinary life with kids, rags, dogs, soon lost to sight among one-storey lime-washed buildings like Arab houses.

The penitentiary had finally shrunk to no more than a yellowish smear when after running alongside the Aniene's dusty banks a while straight ahead opened up a great expanse of meadows sloping down to the wide river basin dotted everywhere, like graveyards, with flowers, a chestnut horse with an astonishingly long neck foraging among the flowers, and far off in the distance, spread out along the entire horizon, Rome.

Before that vision of Rome—or more precisely the Tiber districts from Monte Sacro and Pietralata right over to distant Tor de' Schiavi, Prenestino, and Centocelle, with the thousands of houses like shoeboxes, and the shanties and grim towers—the bus at last came to a standstill.

'Hey, Clippie,' said Claudio, a free man again, 'how about our tickets?'

'Any time,' said the conductor.

'Hang on, what's it cost for one?'

'Twenty lire, to you.'

'No kidding! Where'm I supposed to find twenty lire?'

'Pal, are you asking me?'

'Maybe I don't happen to feel like paying.'

'Suit yourself, son, you're the one who'll cop it.'

'Oh come on, Cla', pay up,' put in his mate Sergio.

'Here, can't a man haggle a bit?' said Claudio. 'Okay mister, make it thirteen.'

'Bloody hell, sonny, you're asking for it, no mistake!' burst out the conductor.

Sergio was fed up too. 'Cut it out, Cla', just give him his forty.'

'Whoa, isn't he the big tough guy!' said the conductor. 'Left your pistols at home, did you, boy?'

'We're a bit hard up and all,' confessed Claudio. 'He's had no work in two years, and I'm just out of the glasshouse.'

And seeing he was just out of the glasshouse, Claudio was over the moon, savouring the first delights of life on the outside, in fact for want of an ATAC* clippie or some other smart arse he'd have picked a fight with a stone just to hear the sound of his own voice. Grandly he extracted the forty lire from his wallet, took the tickets, and headed up the aisle between the seats with the giddy look of a punch-drunk boxer, followed leisurely by Sergio gazing wearily round the place out of that African face of his.

'Let's park ourselves here, eh Ser'?' said Claudio.

'Let's park ourselves here,' said Sergio.

From down the other end of the bus the conductor put in: 'A day to celebrate, eh?'

---

* The Rome bus company

'That's right,' admitted Claudio.

'Celebrate? Celebrate what? When we couldn't even tip the blind man on the corner!' said Sergio, musing grimly into space.

'Leave off,' retorted his companion. 'You go on like that because you've never been in there! Better skint for a year feeding with the friars, if you ask me, than a single day in that place...'

'Stands to reason,' commented the philosopher down there with his poncy hat over his eyes, sorting out the small change.

All at once Claudio and Sergio were up on their feet hurling themselves at the driver's window, hammering on the glass. The driver, who with a pencil tucked behind his ear had been loftily consulting the timetable and doing a bit of mental arithmetic, half inclined his yellow-black face and coldly eyed the two badly dressed louts. But they were far too carried away to realize that among everyone at liberty in this world there could be some who didn't give a toss for freedom and what's more were also pretty pissed off. Ignoring the driver's sour look they good-naturedly signalled to him to get moving, start the engine, turn the ignition.

Behind his window, rigid as a holy image under glass, the driver dead-eyed them a while more, then abruptly raised his forearm to bring his right hand with bunched fingers level with his mouth and nose and wagged it there in a succinct and insolent what-the-fuck interrogative.

Not even when treated to the great Neapolitan gesture of national one-upmanship did the two lads relent.

Claudio hollered: 'Hey driver, at least pretend to start her up!'

'Yeah, or drop dead,' persisted Sergio.

And the conductor from the back of the bus: 'Huh, he could flatten you two, no bother.'

Then what? Three girls in the flashiest ready-made print frocks on sale in Piazza Vittorio came running up the road from the direction of the penitentiary, all of a fluster for fear they'd miss the bus, faces as red as ripe watermelons.

Seeing the driver didn't turn a hair, the two lads stuck their heads and shoulders and arms out the window, feasting their eyes on all that miraculous crumpet bobbing along under the sun as soft as butter.

'Step on it, girls!' yelled Claudio, 'we're off any moment.'

And Sergio: 'Hell, they can move. We'll show them what!'

At which point the conductor struck up:

> *'Stuck in the jailhouse and mamma she's dying...*
> *Wish I too could die 'fore the sun goes down,*
> *Hey mister turnkey, mister turnkey hey!'*

'Oy, Clippie,' shouted Claudio, 'you trying to take the piss?'

'*Stuck in the jailhouse...*' resumes the conductor.

'Man, he's off again.'

The three girls clambered aboard, flushed and gasping inside the bus, all chuffed to have made it. They looked at each other and burst out laughing, then bit by bit their breathlessness and the contagion of laughter passed and they went and sat down on the battered seats, fanning themselves with their hands.

Claudio and Sergio went and sat nearby and began making up to them, and who can blame them seeing you could have said of those three lasses, like the great poet of Rome*:

> *O my lord, what a chicken broth they'd make,*
> *If I could get my claws on them I'd rake*
> *Not just all their feathers off, I'd skin them!*

But it was the bus that showed them what, for it suddenly shook right through, and jangling like a heap of scrap in complete contrast to the driver's officious expression, careered off through the wide fields packed

---

* Giuseppe Gioachino Belli (1791–1863), who wondrously accommodated the classic Italian sonnet form to the unrefined dialect and sentiments of the Roman populace of his time. (See note to Tale 14.)

with poppies and marguerites down the road for Casal dei Pazzi.

To right and left flew by the rich pastures fattened by the Aniene sizzling dark and warm under the sun, and the little half-finished houses all lived in already, and the fancy villas, the old farm buildings ...

'Listen, Se', said Claudio, 'how's Inesse making out?'

'Why ask, Cla'?' answered Sergio. 'Same as ever. When I see her I feel like breaking her face ...'

'Who's she seeing now?'

'Palletta like.'

'Palletta who?'

'Old Mamma Anita's son, you know, her with the stall at Piazza Vittorio ... Short ginger bloke, well built, how can I say ...'

'Ah, I get you. And she's taken up with that runt?'

'What do you expect? But he'll not last long ...'

'She still come off work at six?'

'Yeah.'

'I'll be there tonight.'

'Don't make me mad. What's she got you fancy so much?'

'Look, I just fancy her ...'

With a big grin all over his face Claudio fell to thinking about meeting up with Inesse that evening, and if not her then some other girl from San Lorenzo he'd known since boyhood, it was all the same. As if he was all alone on the bus he settled himself in his seat and burst into song...

> '*Stuck in the jailhouse and mamma she's dying...*
> *Wish I too could die 'fore the sun goes down,*
> *Hey mister turnkey, mister turnkey hey!*'

Chin tucked into his shoulders so the sinews in his neck stretched taut, nostrils flaring and falling above a mouth displaying its entire set of horsey dentures, he rolled his head slowly from side to side to wring out all the passion in his singing.

At the Ponte Mammolo stop the bus filled up with people. Then it joined the Tiburtina highway, crossed the Aniene, and headed straight for Rome.

Next to the two toughs, ostentatiously perusing the *Corriere dello Sport,* had come to stand a young man with a Rudi hairstyle and white shoes, the ones all full of pinholes, and a suit with big black and white stripes over a yellow sports jumper. Claudio looked him over a while, scarcely believing his eyes, taking in all the novelties in fashion this summer. Then, after a good long gander, he sat up and nudged Sergio who was sprawled beside him humming to himself with his neckerchief knotted gangster-style under his glistening dusky face, just as Caravaggio might have painted him.

'Know what, Se'?' said Claudio, 'I'm going to get me one of them shirts with all the holes everyone's wearing, and a pair of them white shoes and all...'

'Bloody hell, fancy being the flash dresser now, eh? Well, good on you...'

'Yeah, good on me, good on me... I've been starved longer than I can stand...'

He bit his knuckles hard, and groaning 'mmhm' eyed up two hot numbers sitting across the aisle, then slowly his gaze adjusted to something far beyond them, outside the window...

'Remember that time, Se?' he said wistfully.

'What time?'

'Right here, when we were kids...'

'What of it?'

'The circus, over at Pietralata, after we took off...'

Ahead, over to the left, past hillocks and gullies towered the Pietralata fortress with a load of Bersaglieri in red fezzes milling around outside, and a bugler in the middle of the yard sounding the call to the cookhouse.

Sergio and Claudio when they were just kids had come this way after running away from home, as Claudio fondly recalled, and they'd hung around here a couple of weeks with empty bellies or at best an onion to chew or some peaches nicked from the street market, and a bit of pork rind pinched from some old grannie's shopping bag...They'd run off like that, just for the hell of it, and scrounged smokes off the Bersaglieri...Then they'd found a place to kip under a watermelon vendor's tent, on top of the melons, and the melon man had a pig out by Bagni di Tivoli, and seeing they'd looked after his melons so well he sent them off to mind the pig, that is the pig and the rabbit...How scary it was inside the hut at night in the deserted countryside, they'd slept with a mallet under their heads...Then one morning the melon man's mum showed up and sent them off into Bagni for some bread, and soon as they were out the way she'd scoffed the rabbit, they'd found its tiny bones buried just outside the hut...

Back in Pietralata, seeing the melon man sent them packing on account of the rabbit, they'd got work in a circus—with the lions!—beating off hordes of local kids desperate for the job...And one evening Rondella, the Maremma mare, had broken out and they'd given chase over the fields and rubbish tips along the banks of the Aniene...

At the end of the Tiburtina the bus crossed over the railway and the shrill of trains and docked amid the general hurly-burly of the Portonaccio terminus. Pale white in the greater white of the day shone the graveside lamps in the Verano cemetery. The 11 was just about to leave. Claudio and Sergio scrambled off the bus and hooting and laughing cut through the crowds to leap onto the tram as it was moving, and stayed outside on the footboard shouting their heads off while the old wagon clattered and clanked up the long avenue skirting the great cemetery wall on its way to San Lorenzo.

In their filthy clothes, with the air of their own district blowing through their hair, clinging on behind a bunch of other folk crowded on the footboard, they were flying homewards. God, life is beautiful, not for the dickheads but for the guys who know how to look after themselves, like the two of them. And while they kicked up a racket Claudio was thinking of himself in his holey shirt and natty white shoes at the Ambra Jovinelli music hall or the big dance floor in Ostia, with Inesse or some other girl in tow to complete the picture of his splendour...

Meantime, in the glassy light under the mighty Verano walls they passed a few couples or an old man, or a toddler on the saddle of his trike with his toes on the ground straining to propel himself up the slope...And the pair of them, hands cupped to their mouths, taunted them all.

'Hey laddie, little laddie, push, push, push...'

'Wow, a couple of years and you'll be a smasher!'

'Watcha, wiggle-bum...'

'Don't listen to him, then say it was me...'

'With that face you'll never get a husband.'

'Hey-up, lad, why bust your guts?'

'Don't give up now, you're almost there...'

'Oh yeah, oh yeah, he'll never rent to you...'

And now here come the first brown houses of San Lorenzo, the first reddish streets, and down there at the far end of the road the Santa Bibiana archway shiny white and getting bigger all the time, and the old public gardens packed with a grand parade of the finest bands of young people in San Lorenzo, all high-spirited, all dressed up for the evening, and the benches and the flower beds and all the greenery of every summer that ever was.

The New Thérèse

Giacomo Casanova

My last day in Florence I passed with my dear Thérèse, both of us vowing to write to each other regularly and without fail in all the time to come. I left next day, and reached Rome within thirty-six hours.

It was one hour after midnight. The walled city can be entered at any time, though foreigners must first call at the customs house which is always open, where their baggage is examined. They are strict only in the matter of books. I had a good thirty, all of them hostile to religion or the virtues it prescribes. Knowing this, I had already resolved to relinquish them without fuss since my first priority was to get some sleep. When he saw all the books the officer inspecting my equipage very courteously asked me to count them and then leave them with him, assuring me that next day he would bring them all to the hotel where I was staying. I consented, and he kept his word. I gave him ten sequins.

After customs I went straight to Piazza di Spagna and the 'Ville de Paris', which was the name of the hotel I had been recommended. Everyone was asleep, but some servants got up and I was ushered into a small ground floor room to wait until a fire had been prepared in the chambers I had been assigned. Finding the chairs all taken up with dresses, petticoats, and chemises, what should I hear but the voice of a girl of whom all that was visible was her head, telling me to sit down on her bed, where another girl was fast asleep. I spy a smiling mouth, and two eyes like burning coals. I sing their praises and beg to be allowed to kiss them. For answer she pulls the coverlet over her head, but I slip my hand inside half down her front, and on discovering she is stark naked, withdraw it, begging her pardon if I seemed overcurious. From her look I felt she was grateful I had been good enough to curb my curiosity.

'And who are you, my pretty angel?'

'I am Thérèse Roland, the proprietor's daughter, and this is my sister.'

'You're seventeen?'

'Not for much longer.'

'I can scarcely wait to see you tomorrow on your feet in my chamber.'

'Are there women in your party?'

'No.'

'Too bad. We never go up to men's rooms.'

'Pull this cover down more, it prevents you speaking.'

'It's so cold.'

'Charming Thérèse, your eyes fair set my soul ablaze.'

She pulls her head under the coverlet once more, I seize the moment and thrust my hand in deep, her knees fly up, I spring, and satisfy myself she is indeed a female angel.

Enough for now. I withdraw my hand, all the while begging her pardon, and note her face is relieved, laughing, inflamed and tinged with just a touch of anger, but also delight. I am about to embark on a sentimental and amorous passionate speech, when a handsome servant girl comes in and asks me to go up.

'Adieu, until tomorrow,' I say to the charming Thérèse, who merely responds by turning over to go back to sleep.

Having ordered luncheon for one o'clock, I retired to bed and slept until midday all the time dreaming of this new Thérèse. My servant Costa informed me that he had found the house where my brother was living, and had left a note there. This was my brother Giovanni, who was then about thirty and in Rome at the art school of the famous Mengs. It was ten years since I had last seen this brother.

I was still at table when he appeared before me. After embracing each other and passing an hour together during which we each briefly recounted our adventures, his slight, mine extraordinary, he concludes that the very first thing I must do is to leave this hotel which is far too expensive and lodge where it will cost me nothing, in the household of the painter Mengs who has an empty apartment. As for board, he tells me a caterer lives in the same street. I retort that I haven't the strength of mind to find lodgings elsewhere because I have fallen in love with one of the hotelier's daughters; and I recount the story of the previous night. He laughs and says it is not love but an infatuation which I can carry on just the same, and I am persuaded. I promise to move in with him next day, and we go out together for a walk round Rome.

I first went over to the Minerva to call on Donna Cecilia, only to be told she had died two years before. I asked where her daughter Donna Angelica was living, went straight there and was very poorly received, to the point of her claiming she barely remembered having met me. I left, and with no regrets, for to me she seemed to have grown quite ugly. I found out where the doctor was living, the printer's son who was said to have married Barbaruccia, but then decided to call on him some other day, as also on my good friend padre Georgi who now enjoyed a great reputation in Rome. My brother then took me to Signora Cherufini's, where I found myself in a house of truly exquisite taste. He introduced me, the mistress received me in the best Roman fashion, I found her appealing, her daughters even more so; however, I found their very mixed bag of worshippers far too numerous, an infuriatingly superficial bunch, and the young ladies, one of whom was as pretty as a peach, seemed far too attentive to all and sundry. Asked an interesting question, I replied in a manner which should have elicited another, and instead it received no response at all. But what do I care? In this house I realized I stood to lose all my intrinsic worth, and this on account of the quality of the person who had presented me. I hear a priest saying to another who is looking my way:

'It's Casanova's brother.'

I tell him he would do better to say it is Casanova who is my brother, and he answers it makes no difference. Another priest says it makes all the difference, we talk, and become good friends. It is in fact the illustrious padre Winckelmann, who was murdered twelve years later in Trieste.

Cardinal Alessandro Albani arrives, Winckelmann presents me, and His Eminence who is almost blind tells me many things, none worth hearing. Most of all that he knows I am the very same man who escaped from the Piombi*, and he barefacedly tells me he is astonished I have the audacity to come to Rome where the least

* The supposedly impregnable prison above the Ducal Palace in Venice from which Casanova had escaped four years previously.

request from the Venetian state inquisitors will prompt a papal *ordine santissimo* obliging me to depart. Soured by this warning, I answer that not by this should he judge my audacity, since in Rome I risk nothing.

'It is rather the state inquisitors', I inform him, 'who should be deemed audacious were they to dare to issue a summons against me, for they are in no position to declare on account of what crime they deprived me of my liberty.'

This curt and forthright reply silences the cardinal, who ashamed of having taken me for an idiot does not address another word to me. I never set foot in the Cherufini house again. We returned to the 'Ville de Paris' with padre Winckelmann whom my brother persuaded to stay and sup with us.

My host Roland, being well acquainted with my brother, paid us a visit during supper. I informed the man, who was from Avignon and a very good fellow, that I was vexed at having to leave his house to go and live with my brother, because I had fallen in love with his daughter Thérèse after only speaking to her for a quarter of an hour and having seen no more than her head.

'You saw her in bed, I believe.'

'Precisely. Now I should wish to see her up on her two feet. Would you be so good as to have her come up for the occasion?'

'With pleasure.'

She came up, plainly delighted at her father's summons. She had a trim figure and a gay and candid air, and might almost have passed for pretty although her eyes were the only striking thing about her face. My enthusiasm diminished; but my brother, without saying anything to me, set his cap at her so firmly that a year later he let himself be ensnared. The young Thérèse certainly knew how to get herself a husband, and two years later he took her with him to Dresden, where five years after I saw her with a babe-in-arms. She died, thin as a rake, ten years later.

The Shirt on the Wall

Erri De Luca

Amore e Roma: crossword devisers call it a palindrome, a phrase which reads the same in reverse. Love and Rome: both happened to me with the force of absolute novelty far from where I was born. Eighteen years from first to last I'd lived in Naples, like a eunuch, never having loved any girl in the neighbourhoods where I grew up. Only on the island opposite, love flowered one summer for a girl from Rome. So when at eighteen I fled the south which made and moulded me, that was the city I went to because some love remained, not much, but enough to point in that direction someone adrift from his centre, equidistant from every point of arrival.

Now she was a grown woman, she studied architecture and she smoked. I've never been able to handle tobacco or kindred substances, and I wanted no more to do with studies, houses, family, city. I was both dispossessed and possessed. Some decisions taken at a tender age never buckle, lodged too deep in God knows what bone in the body.

Like most uninvited arrivals, Rome for me was first of all the railway station. In its vicinity I found a succession of beds in boarding houses among total strangers. Never have I felt so alone, the perfect state in which to fall in love or go under. I didn't drown because all around me young people were fired by a strange fury, political, but nothing to do with the official parties. Informal, irregular, with no use for party cards and conferences, its constituency the street, sit-ins its parliament. Up against the police, the courts, prison. I went with them so did not break. And I fell in love, not with the first girl, the one on the island, but her sister, sixteen and awesome in her strength of will and beauty. Her hands were scabbed by some affliction, the only one I've ever loved. I venerated those cracked hands, red and sore, though she never believed me. Had it been leprosy I'd have licked them to get it on my tongue, were it death I would have wanted it. Anything less, love is nothing.

The year was 1969, grimmer and longer than the experimental '68. Some young people started identifying with the biographies of early twentieth-century revolutionaries. Many more of us learned to weep tear-gas tears and to brave baton charges, bloody heads, and comical journeys cooped like chickens in Black Marias. Who I was or what I had to say for myself—zero. I was from nothing and nowhere. I was one of the many and at times not so many, when lined up in a police yard for a cold-blooded reprisal beating from the men in uniform. I was one, even less than one. Yet I loved. I loved the girl with silken hair snapped in profile some spring day by the Roman Forum, one of our walks. I loved the girl with shoulders broad enough to meet me head-on, like a storm wave lifts a boat.

I counted my every muscle and bone—how puny I was; I counted my years, my cash—how could I ever keep her? She grew up all through that summer I lived on prickly pears and a feast of kisses invoked and granted. All I craved was the portal of kisses. More than liberty I hungered for the scalding minute when four lips catch their breath and meet to taste themselves on each other and mingle to become one another's.

She lived at home, I in shared lodgings, so we seldom met alone. Kisses are not the prelude to further tenderness, they are the high point. From their summit we can fall to hands grappling, loins thrusting, but that is to be swept away. Only kisses, like the cheeks of fish, are good. We held the bait between our lips, we took it together.

Winter came and I had a tiny rented room of my own, my first, near Villa Ada. I'd nailed a shirt to the wall. Unbutton it and inside were two photographs, hers of course. She came to me secretly, but found me sick. A cloying, crushing fever was chilling on my skin. Opening the door, I had to cling to the handle. She held me tight, like hugging winter, while I shivered and chittered, marble in my feet. There was no heating and I only noticed it then. Rigid with cold, I longed not for blood but chocolate in my veins. She held me tight inside her fleecy sheepskin coat. She shut the door with the heel of her shoe and pushed me backwards towards the bed without loosening her embrace.

She laid me down and undressed to a white slip, light as air. She came inside the dark of the blankets and covered all my body with hers. I lay under her, trembling with happiness and cold. Every part of us matched, hand with hand, foot on foot, hair in hair, navel to navel, nose by nose, breathing only through them, our mouths fused. It was more than kissing, missing halves were twinned again. If a resurrection technique exists she applied it. She absorbed all my cold and fever, raw matter to be reworked within her body and returned to me as the weight of love. Her love pressed mine and mine held hers, as earth holds snow. If an alliance exists between female and male I lived it then.

It lasted an hour, longer than any forever. Before leaving she laughed at the shirt on the wall. That's my buttoned crucifixion. I didn't tell her she was inside. She never returned. Winter drove us apart. She had come to leave me and instead lay down to cure me. The best things about love happen by chance but are only understood long after. I'd thought her visit was the start of an even vaster together, instead it was the finish. I believed in a time to come and it was the time before. In my head kept hammering the syllables of the Spanish poet, heavy as a bell:

'To go north he went south. | He thought wheat was water | he was wrong. | He thought the sea was sky | and night the morning. | He was wrong. | That the stars were dew | and summer a snowfall | he was wrong.' A singer in our group had set these lines to music. Like salt, music keeps things longer. I had been wrong, and very slowly I recovered from love and its fits of happiness. I got used to the city, a conduit leaking love from every fountain. I walked through it with eyes I'll have again when I am old: Villa Ada was full of mothers and children who meant nothing to me.

Around that time the university canteen workers and students had decided anyone could eat there, even with- out a pass. With no more than three hundred lire I was set up for the day. The time of fever and hunger was over, I ate in Via De Lollis together with the many who were invent- ing new rights, wresting them from the powerful. The city took to us and we took over her streets and suburbs, surrounded by troops we no longer feared.

Once in a while at some demonstration amid crowds of our people I'd see her again. She had married very soon. She was becoming a woman, one woman, and once she had contained so many and I had known them all. I'd loved her many girls who tried on grown women's dresses in the year of kisses. Later I loved others mistaking them for her all over again. I needed that mistake to be able to fall in love.

I quit the rented room on impulse a few years later, not even taking a pair of underpants with me. The shirt nailed up by the cuffs remained there, ownerless. Perhaps it's the only way to go, speedily, as though absconding. But all this was later, when the mutual hatreds hardened and our blood and that of others hardly had time to dry.

In the ferment of new griefs I forgot the girl who held me tight inside her coat and left me to become a woman. Rome was full of war. Those who say it was all a delusion really abandoned the field. There was no obligation to fight but there was reason to. That generation of the many had no need of recruiting sergeants, it was sufficient unto itself. It never aspired to be the majority, the efforts of a minority combined to shift the load. I don't miss it because it is never out of my thoughts. Neither do I miss that hour of resurrection beneath the body of the girl I loved. I was vouchsafed that hour without end, I lived it.

Cola di Rienzo

Anonymous Roman

Cola di Rienzo was of low birth. His father was a tavern keeper named Rienzo. His mother was named Maddalena and made a living washing clothes and carrying water. He was born in the district of Regola. His house was by the river among the millers on the road to Regola, behind San Tommaso, below the temple of the Jews. From boyhood he was nourished on the milk of eloquence, a good grammarian, even better rhetorician, a great scholar. Oh, what a fast reader he was! He knew all Livy, Seneca and Cicero, and Valerius Maximus. He loved to recount all the marvels of Julius Caesar. Every day he pondered the marble carvings lying about Rome. No one else could read the old inscriptions. He translated all the ancient writings. All those marble sculptures he interpreted rightly. Oh, how often he would say: 'Where are these good Romans? Where is their supreme justice? Would I could have lived when they lived!'

He was a handsome man, and on his lips was always a smile in some ways fantastical. He was a notary. It happened one of his brothers was killed and his death was not avenged. He could not help him. For long he thought how to avenge his brother's blood. For long he thought how to set to rights misrule in the city of Rome. To this end he went to Avignon on an embassy to Pope Clement on behalf of the Thirteen Good Men of Rome.* His oratory was so persuasive and beautiful that Pope Clement was at once captivated. He wanted to see him every day. So then Cola spoke up and said the barons of Rome are highwaymen, they abet murder, robbery, adultery, every evil, they revel in the ruin of their city. The pope was angered at the powerful. Then, at the instigation of Cardinal Giovanni della Colonna, he fell into such disgrace, such poverty, such poor health that he was only good for hospital. In his undershirt he lay out in the sun like a snake. The man who thrust him down raised him up, Cardinal Giovanni

---

* The government of 'Thirteen Good Men' was one of many short-lived attempts to set up a communal administration in Rome in opposition to the feudal barons during the long period of economic depression and lawlessness caused by the transfer of the pope and the curia to Avignon (1308–77). The other absent overlord invoked by Cola was the Holy Roman Emperor, though this was more a matter of unrealistic nostalgia since none had actually resided in Rome for 350 years and their power outside central Europe was negligible.

presented him to the pope once more. Again he was in favour, was made notary of the Chamber of Rome, and received many favours and benefits. He went back to Rome a happy man. And in his heart he planned revenge.

When back from court he began to exercise his office prudently, and at close hand he could see the thievery of the dogs of the Capitol, the cruelty and injustice of the nobles. He saw the great Commune in danger and no good citizen who cared to save it. So one time in the court of justice in Rome in front of all the councillors he rose to his feet and said, 'You are not good citizens, you suck the blood of the poor and refuse to help them.' Then he admonished the rulers and officials for not working for the good of their own city of Rome. At the end of this fine speech one of the Colonna—Andreuccio di Normanno, chamberlain at the time—got to his feet and gave him a resounding slap. Then a senate scribe—Tommaso di Fortifiocca was his name—stood up and blew a raspberry. That was what he gained for speaking out.

Cola di Rienzo did not use a goose quill to write, he said his office was so noble that his pen must be silver. Not long after, he harangued the people in a fine address in the vernacular which he delivered in San Giovanni Laterano. On the wall behind the choir he had a large and magnificent metal tablet set up covered in antique lettering which he alone could read and interpret. He had pictures painted round this tablet showing how the Roman senate granted authority to the Emperor Vespasian. And there, in the centre of the church, he had a place of assembly constructed of timbers with raised wooden stalls for seating. And he decorated it with carpets and drapes. Here he convened nearly all the powerful men in Rome, among them Stefano della Colonna and his son Gianni Colonna, one of the shrewdest and most gallant men in Rome. Many learned men were also present, judges and canon lawyers, many others in authority. Amid all these fine people Cola di Rienzo mounted the rostrum. He wore a German gown and a cape and hood of fine white linen. On his head he wore a white hat. Round the rim were gold crowns, the foremost split in half. From the peak of the hat came a silver blade and its tip struck the crown and cut it in two. Boldly he mounted. When silence fell he began his splendid address, beautifully worded, and said Rome had been hurled to the ground and could not see where she lay prostrate because her eyes had been put out. Her eyes were the pope and the emperor, lost to Rome through the iniquity of her people. Then he said, 'Now marvel at the grandeur of the senate which conceded authority to the emperor.' Then he had a document read out in which were written all the rights which the Roman people invested in the Emperor Vespasian. First, that Vespasian could make laws and confederations with whatsoever nation or people he saw fit; also he could promote men to the position of duke and king and likewise depose and degrade them; he could destroy cities and rebuild them; he could divert the courses of rivers; he could impose and remit taxes at will. All these things the Roman people granted the Emperor Vespasian, just as they had conceded them to Tiberius Caesar.

When the document had been read out, all these points, he said, 'Gentlemen, such was the majesty of the Roman people that they granted the emperor his authority. Now we have lost it.' And he concluded, saying, 'May you live in peace with one another.' But then he appended these words: 'Gentlemen, I know that many speak ill of me for these things I do and say, and for why? For envy. But I thank God three things consume themselves. The first is lust, the second fire, the third is envy.' At the end of this address he stepped down and was praised by all.

In these same days, invited to banquet with the grandees of Rome and Gianni Colonna, the barons would mock his speechifying. They made him get to his feet and say his fill. And he said: 'I shall be a great lord or emperor. All these barons I shall persecute. This one I'll hang, this one I'll decapitate.' He judged them all. The barons could not contain their laughter.

Now Cola di Rienzo becomes bolder, though not without fear, and together with the papal vicar he occupies the palace on the Capitol in the year of our Lord 1347. He was protected by a force of some one hundred armed men. A great multitude of the people gathered, and in the assembly hall he delivered a mighty oration on the misery and servitude of the people of Rome. He said that for love of the pope and for the salvation of the Roman people he was exposing his person to danger. Then he had a document read out which contained his ordinances for the good state. Conte, son of Cecco Mancino, read it in summary. Here are some of its articles:

> *Whoever kills another person shall himself be killed, no exception made.*
>
> *Lawsuits to be settled within maximum fifteen days.*
>
> *Every district of Rome shall maintain one hundred foot soldiers and twenty-five cavalrymen at the expense of the Commune.*
>
> *The Treasury of the Commune of Rome shall assist orphans and widows.*
>
> *To protect merchants a ship shall be maintained to guard all Roman marshes, lakes, and seashores.*
>
> *All moneys from hearth tax, salt tax, city gates and tolls, and fines, where applicable, to be spent for the good of the people.*
>
> *No castles, bridges, city gates, or forts to be guarded by any baron, but solely by the leader of the people.*
>
> *No noble may possess a fortress within the city.*
>
> *The barons shall keep roads secure and not harbour robbers and malefactors, and furthermore shall furnish provisions for Rome or be fined one thousand silver marks.*

Many other things were written in this document, and all so delighted the people that all cheered loudly and joyfully proclaimed they wished him to remain as their ruler together with the papal vicar. They further gave him licence to punish, execute, pardon, appoint officers, make laws and treaties with other peoples, and determine borders.

When these things done in Rome came to the ears of Messer Stefano della Colonna, who was in Corneto with the militia to procure grain, he gathered a small band of men and rode in great haste to Rome. When they reached Piazza San Marcello* he declared these things displeased him. Early next morning Cola di Rienzo sent Messer Stefano an edict commanding him to leave Rome. Messer Stefano took the paper and tore it into a thousand pieces, saying, 'If this madman aggravates me anymore I shall have him thrown from the Capitol windows.' When Cola di Rienzo heard this he at once had the great bell rung to sound the alarm. All the populace came out in fury. Great danger threatened. So then Messer Stefano mounted his horse. With a single foot servant he fled from Rome.

Then Cola di Rienzo sent orders to all the barons of Rome to leave the city and go to their castles, and at once this was done. Next day all bridges within the city walls

---

* San Marcello, on the present-day Corso near Piazza Venezia, was the Colonna family church in a neighbourhood dominated by this powerful clan.

were handed over to him. Then Cola di Rienzo appointed his own officers. And now he seizes one man after another: some he hangs, some he beheads without pity. All the troublemakers he condemns ruthlessly. Then he spoke to the people and in the assembly had himself confirmed again and all his actions endorsed, and he asked for the people's approval that he and the papal vicar be called tribunes of the people and liberators.

Out of fear, all the barons swore obedience to him and the good state, and offered their own persons and castles and vassals in aid of the city. He dressed in fiery scarlet. His face and appearance were terrifying. Over the next days the city magistrates came and swore fidelity to him and to work for the good of the state. Then came the notaries and did likewise. Then the merchants. In sum, in good order and in peace, unarmed, every man swore to work for the common good. So then these things began to please all and fighting began to cease. A horrible dread filled the hearts of robbers, murderers, malefactors, adulterers, and all people of bad repute. Every miscreant slunk out of the city, secretly fled. The wicked went in fear of being seized in their homes and dragged off to their doom. So the guilty fled far beyond the borders of the Roman lands. They could look to no man for salvation. They abandoned their houses, fields, vineyards, wives, and children. So then the forests began to rejoice, for not a robber was to be found in them. Oxen began to plough. Pilgrims began to venture out to the sanctuaries. Merchants began to travel again and increase their affairs. The roads were opened. No one dared carry arms. No man did injury to another. The master dared not touch his servant. The tribune watched over everything.

For happiness at such a great thing many wept for joy and prayed God to fortify his heart and mind in his endeavour. The tribune's chief intent was to exterminate the tyrants and destroy them so no trace remained.

At first this man led a very temperate life. Then he began to indulge in dinners and banquets, gorging on diverse dishes and wines and many sweetmeats. Then he had the Capitol palace reinforced between the columns with a palisade and sealed off by timbers. And he ordered all the palisades of the barons of Rome to be torn down, and it was done. He ordered the resulting beams and planks and timbers to be carried to the Capitol at the barons' expense, and it was done. Then he fined each senator one hundred florins, since he wished to use the money to rebuild and restore the Capitol palace. He received one hundred florins from each baron also, but the palace was not restored, though it was begun.

In the Capitol he built a very beautiful chapel, and there he had solemn mass sung with many singers and lights. Then he forced to stand before him, while he sat, all the barons up on their feet with arms folded and their hoods back. Oh, how they trembled where they stood!

This man had a very young and beautiful wife who when she went to St Peter's was accompanied by armed youths. Well-born ladies followed them. Maidservants were kept busy fanning dainty kerchiefs before her face to keep the flies off. He had an uncle called Gianni Varvieri. He was a barber but was made a great lord and called Gianni Roscio. He raced about on horseback accompanied by Roman citizens. All his relatives went about in the same way. He had a widowed sister whom he wanted to marry to a baron with a castle.

As things prospered for him he wanted to be sole ruler, so he dismissed the papal vicar, his colleague, who was from beyond the Alps, a great expert in canon law and bishop of Viterbo. Then he sent an ambassador to the pope to announce the fact. This ambassador, when he returned, said the pope and all the cardinals were much perturbed.

Now I shall tell you how he was made an exalted knight. When the tribune saw that everything proceeded well for him, and that he ruled in peace without opposition, he began to desire the honour of knighthood. And so he was created Knight of the Bath on the vigil of the Feast of the Assumption in mid-August. First he had all the pope's palace and the neighbourhood of San Giovanni Laterano decked out as for a marriage, and many days beforehand had dining tables made from the planks and beams of the stockades of the barons of Rome. And these tables were set up in the whole of the hall of the old palace of Constantine and in the new palace, so everyone who saw them was stupefied. All Rome, men and women, went to San Giovanni. All crowded on top of the porticos to view the celebrations and on the public streets to see the triumph. In front of the tribune walked a man with a drawn sword. Above his head another carried a banner. He himself carried a steel staff in his hand. Many notable people were in his company. He was dressed in a robe of dazzling white silk with stripes in thread of gold.

That evening at dusk he went up into the chapel of Pope Boniface and addressed the people, saying, 'Be it known that tonight I am to be made a knight. Return tomorrow, for you shall hear things which will delight God in heaven and men on earth.' When everyone had departed, divine office was celebrated by the clergy. And after the service he bathed in the basin of the Emperor Constantine, which is made of precious touchstone.* An astonishing thing to report and which gave rise to much comment. A Roman citizen, Messer

* In the baptistery of San Giovanni, believed to have been used a thousand years earlier for the baptism of the Emperor Constantine by Pope Sylvester.

Vico Scuotto, knight, buckled on his sword. Then he slept in a venerable bed in that place called the baptistery of San Giovanni, inside the circle of columns. There he spent the whole night.

At daybreak the tribune rose and dressed in fur-trimmed scarlet, with his sword buckled on by Vico Scuotto and gold spurs as befits a knight. All Rome went to San Giovanni, all the knights and barons and foreigners and citizens, to view Messer Nicola di Rienzo, knight. There was great feasting and rejoicing. Messer Nicola stood adorned as a knight in the chapel of Pope Boniface above the piazza in solemn company. There most solemn mass was sung. Every singer was present, every treasure was on display. In the midst of this solemn ceremony the tribune appeared before the people and spoke in a loud voice, saying, 'We summon Pope Clement to come to Rome, his See.' Then he summoned the college of cardinals. Then the Bavarian.* Then he summoned all the imperial electors of Germany and said: 'I want these men to come to Rome. I want to see they make the right election.' Having issued this summons, letters were immediately drawn up and couriers despatched. After this he drew his sword from its scabbard and struck the sides of the altar in three directions of the

---

* Louis of Bavaria, contender for the title of Holy Roman Emperor.

compass, saying, 'This is mine, this is mine, this is mine'. The papal legate was present at these things. He was like a dumb chock of wood. Stunned at first, he finally protested, shocked at this unprecedented act. He had one of his notaries publicly protest on his behalf that these things were not done by his will, and were without his knowledge and the pope's permission. While the notary was shouting out this protest to the people, Messer Nicola commanded that all trumpets, bugles, kettledrums, and shawms be played, so the notary's voice could not be heard above the greater din. Perverse buffoonery!

Now hear something remarkable. All through that day, from dawn till the ninth hour, from lead pipes inserted in the nostrils of Constantine's bronze horse* poured red wine from the right nostril and from the left water, falling without cease into the brimming basin. All the youths who were thirsty, citizens and strangers, crowded round and drank gleefully. When it became known he had bathed in Constantine's basin and had summoned the pope, people were very troubled and fearful. Some reproached him for presumption, others said he was fantastical, crazy.

---

* The equestrian statue of the Emperor Marcus Aurelius was formerly believed to represent Constantine, the first Christian emperor, and for centuries stood in the piazza outside the Lateran Palace until removed to the Capitol as part of Michelangelo's redesigned Campidoglio.

These various vices led to his downfall and brought him to perdition in the following way. One day he invited Messer Stefano della Colonna to dine with him. When the time came for the meal he had him brought forcibly to the Capitol and held him there. Then he had Pietro di Agabito brought to him, lord of Genazzano, a Roman senator at the time. Lubertiello, too, son of Count Vertuollo, was brought there under force, also a senator. These two senators he had brought to the Capitol as though they were common thieves. He also detained the illustrious young Gianni Colonna, whom only a few days before he had made captain over the Campagna. He also detained Giordano Orsini of Monti, and Messer Rinaldo Orsini. He detained Cola Orsini, master of Castel Sant'Angelo. He detained Count Vertuollo, Messer Orso di Vicovaro degli Orsini, and many other great barons of Rome. All these barons the tribune held in the confines of his prison under guard by what was in effect an act of betrayal, since he had given them to understand he wished to take counsel with some, and dine with others.

When evening came the Roman populace roundly denounced the wickedness of the nobles and extolled the excellence of the tribune. So then Messer Stefano proposed a question: what most befitted a leader of the people, munificence or thrift? There was much discussion. After everyone had had their say Messer Stefano grasped the hem of the tribune's fine robe: 'For you, Tribune, it would be more appropriate to wear the clothes of an honest Franciscan tertiary, not such pompous things.' And so saying he held up the hem of the robe. Cola di Rienzo took umbrage at this.

By now it was evening. He had all the nobles rounded up and put under guard. Messer Stefano was shut in the hall of the court of justice. All night he spent without a bed. He paced back and forth, beat on the door, begged the guards to open up. The guards did not listen. A cruel thing was done to him all that pitiless night.

A new day dawns. The tribune had resolved to behead them all in the assembly hall to free the Roman people once and for all. He ordered the walls of the hall to be draped with red and white silk, and it was done. This was to signify blood. Then he had the bell rung, and the people gathered. Then he sent a confessor, a friar minor, to each of the barons so they could do penance and take the Body of Christ. When the barons heard what was to happen and the tolling of the bell, they became so petrified they could not speak, they did not know what to do. Most of them humbled themselves and did penance and took communion. Messer Rinaldo Orsini and some others, because they had eaten fresh figs early in the morning, could not take communion. Messer Stefano della Colonna refused to confess or take communion. He said he was not prepared and had not settled his affairs.

Meantime certain Roman citizens, perturbed by the sentence he wanted to impose, dissuaded him with sweet and flattering words. In the end they changed the tribune's mind and he abandoned his plan.

It was the third hour. All the barons, grieving like damned souls, came down to the assembly hall. The trumpets were sounded as though the barons were to be executed in front of the people. The tribune, now of a different mind, mounted the rostrum and delivered a fine speech. It was based on the passage from the Lord's Prayer, 'Forgive us our trespasses.' Then he pardoned the barons and said they now wanted to serve the people, and he reconciled them with the people. One by one they bowed their heads to the people. Some he made patricians, some he made prefects of the office of provisions, another a duke of Tuscany, another duke of Campagna. And he presented them each with a fine robe trimmed with fur and a banner embroidered with golden ears of grain. Then he had them dine with him and rode through Rome with all of them following. Then he let them go on their way safely.

These actions greatly displeased the thoughtful. People said, 'This man has lit a fire and flame he will never be able to put out.' And I give him this proverb: 'He who wishes to fart and tightens his arse wears out his buttocks.'

Then the tribune began to be hated. People spoke ill of him and said his arrogance was too much. Then he began to become horribly wicked and abandon all pretence of acting honourably. He dressed like an Asian tyrant. Now it became apparent he wished to tyrannize. He began extorting money from the abbeys. He seized whoever had money and took it from them, and then swore them to silence. He called public assemblies less often for fear of the wrath of the people. And he gained colour and weight, and ate better, slept better. Then he dismissed the prefect because he was infirm and held his son hostage. Then the people began to desert him, and fewer barons attended court. Then he imposed the salt tax, needing to raise money for the army.

Now I shall tell you about the tribune's death. He had imposed a tax on wine and other things. He called it 'subsidy'. The Romans were as timid as sheep. They dared not speak their minds. They feared this tribune like a demon. In council he got his every whim, no councillor dared oppose him. He would laugh and weep at the same time, break into tears and sighs even as he laughed, so volatile and fickle was his will. Sometimes he wept, sometimes he was hysterical with joy. Then he started arresting people. He detained one man after another and ransomed them. Murmuring against him stealthily began to spread through Rome. So to protect himself he raised fifty foot soldiers from each district of the city, ready for any emergency. He paid them nothing. Promised every day, kept them hoping.

It was the month of September, the eighth day. The morning found Cola di Rienzo in his bed. He had washed his face in Greek wine. Suddenly a cry was heard, 'Long live the people, long live the people!' At this people came out onto the streets from all sides. The cry grew louder, the numbers swelled. Armed men gathered at the market crossroads coming from Sant'Angelo and Ripa, others from Colonna and Trevi. As they assembled a new cry went up: 'Death to the traitor Cola di Rienzo! Death!' Now the young men move to the attack in a fury, the very ones he had enlisted to stand by him. Not all districts turned out, only those mentioned. They ran to the Capitol palace. There they were joined by great numbers of people, men, women, and children. They threw stones, they made a great clamour, they surrounded the palace on all sides, behind as well as in front, saying, 'Death to the traitor who made the tax! Death!' Terrible was their wrath.

The tribune did nothing to defend himself. He did not sound the bell, he did not summon his men. At first he said, 'They say "Long live the people", and we say the same. We are here to raise up the people. I have my own militia. The letter from the pope confirming my appointment has come. I only have to announce it in council.' When finally he saw the shouting bode no good, he was very afraid, most of all because he had been deserted by every living person on the Capitol. Judges, notaries, soldiers, all had looked to save their skins. Only he and three other people remained, one being Locciolo Pellicciaro, his kinsman.

When the tribune saw the tumult of the people kept growing, saw he was forsaken and defenceless, he was sore afraid. He asked the three of them what to do. Searching for a remedy, he took heart and said: 'It will not go their way, by my troth.' Then he armed himself like a knight for the fight, donning his helmet, breastplate and fauld, and greaves. He took up the banner of the people and stepped out alone on the balcony of the great upper hall. He raised his hand, motioning for silence since he wished to speak. Without doubt if they had listened to him he would have broken them and changed their minds, they would have been routed. But the Romans did not want to hear him. They acted like pigs. They threw stones, fired arrows. They ran up with lighted torches to burn the gate. The volleys of arrows and darts drove him off the balcony. One dart struck his hand. Then he seized the banner and stretched out the silk in both hands. He displayed the letters of gold*, the arms of the citizens of Rome, as if to say, 'You will not let me speak. But see, I am a citizen and one of the people like you. I love you, and if you kill me you kill yourselves, for we are all Romans.' This tactic was of no avail. It only made the mindless people worse. 'Death to the traitor!' they cried.

Unable to endure it any more, he looked for some other way to save himself. He was afraid to stay in the upper hall because also a prisoner there was Messer Bettrone de Narba, to whom he had done great injury. He was afraid he might kill him with his bare hands. He could see him signalling to the people. He decided to leave the upper hall and get away from Messer Bettrone for his own safety. So then he took tablecloths from the tables and tied them around his waist and had himself lowered down into the courtyard in front of the prison. The prisoners in the prison saw everything. He took the keys and kept them on him. He could not trust the prisoners.

Up in the hall remained Locciolo Pellicciaro who every so often went out onto the balconies gesturing and calling out to the people, saying, 'Now he's coming down at the back!' and they went round to the back of the palace where he was coming. Then he turned back to the tribune and encouraged him and told him not to fear. Then he

---

* SPQR: Senatus Populusque Romanorum, the Senate and People of Rome.

returned to the people and made similar signals: 'Look, now he's out the back, now he's gone down the back.' He told them where and gave the order. Locciolo killed him. Locciolo Pellicciaro destroyed the liberty of the people, who can never find a leader. Only through that man could they achieve freedom. If Locciolo had done no more than encourage him assuredly he would not have died, for the hall was on fire, and soon after the bridge of the stairway fell in. No one could have got to him. The day was advancing. The people of Regola and the other districts would have come, swelled the numbers, changed minds, because they were of a different opinion. Everyone would have gone home, or there would have been a great battle. But Locciolo barred that hope.

In despair, the tribune left it to fortune to determine his fate. Standing in the courtyard outside the Chancellery, now he put on his helmet, now he took it off. This was because he was in two minds. His first notion was to die honourably in full armour with sword in hand among the people in the manner of a lordly and imperious figure. And this he showed when he put on his helmet and took up his weapons. His other notion was to save himself and not perish. And this he showed when he took off his helmet. These two desires battled in his mind. The will to escape and live prevailed. He was a man like any other, he was scared to die. Once he had decided it was better to live by any means he could he came up with both the means and the way, a shameful and faint-hearted way.

By now the Romans had built a fire against the first gate, wood, oil, and pitch. The gate was burning. The loggia roof was blazing. The second gate caught fire and the floor fell in and the beams dropped one by one. The noise was horrible. The tribune thought if he was disguised he could pass through the fire, mingle with the others, and survive. This was his final hope. He could see no other way. So he took off his noble insignia and laid down his weapons. It is painful to recall. He cut off his beard and painted his face with a lot of blacking. There was a small cabin nearby where the gatekeeper slept. He went in and took a cloak of rough cloth, of the sort worn by herdsmen in the Campagna. He put on that coarse cloak. Then over his head he pulled some bedding from the bed and disguised like that he went down. He goes through the burning gate, goes down the stairway past the terror of the collapsing floor, passes safely through the last gate. The fire did not touch him. He mingled with the others. Being in disguise, he disguised his voice too. He spoke countrywise and said, 'Daan, daan wi' the trettor!' If he could pass the last stairway he was free. People's attention was all up there on the palace. He passed through the last gate but someone barred his way and recognized him, took hold of him, and said, 'Stop there. Where are you going?' He pulled the feather bolster off his head, but was struck even more by the splendour of the bracelets he wore. They were gold, they did not look like something belonging to a low fellow. Then, now he was discovered, the tribune revealed himself openly, showed he was indeed himself. There was no going back. There was no way out now but to throw himself on their mercy, rely on the will of others.

Seized by the arms, he was brought unresisting up all the stairs to the place of the lion, where others had heard their sentence, where he had sentenced others. Brought there, a great silence fell. No man dared touch him. There he sat for little short of an hour, his beard cut, his face black as a baker's, in an undershirt of green silk, unbelted, with gold shoulder straps, in the sky-blue stockings barons wear. His arms folded. In that silence he turned his face, looked this way and that. Then Cecco dello Viecchio grabbed a rapier and stabbed him in the stomach. He was the first. The second was a notary from Trevi who struck him over the head with his sword. Then another struck, and another, and more and still more. Some stab, some tell him what he has coming. He did not utter a sound. The first blow killed him, he felt no pain.

A man came with a rope and bound his feet together. They pushed him over and dragged him away, it tore the skin off him. In that state they ran him through till he was a sieve. Everyone had sport with him. You would have thought a plenary indulgence had been proclaimed. In this fashion he was dragged over to San Marcello. There he was hung by his feet from a small balcony. His head had gone. It lay in splinters along the road where they had dragged him. His innards hung out, all fatty. He was horribly fat, white like bloodstained milk. He was so fat he looked like an outsize buffalo or cow at the slaughterhouse. There he hung two days and one night. Boys threw stones at him.

The third day, on orders from Iugurta and Sciarra Colonna he was hauled off to Campo dell'Augusta.* There all the Jews were gathered in a great multitude, not one was absent. They built a bonfire of dry cardoons. Because of all the fat he burned easily. The Jews worked busily, hurrying about, their sleeves pushed back. They stirred up the cardoons to make him burn. And so that body was burned and reduced to dust, not a speck remained.

Thus perished Cola di Rienzo, who made himself august tribune of Rome, who wanted to be the Romans' champion. This man was killed in the year of Our Lord 1354, the eighth day of September, the third hour.

---

* The area round the mausoleum of the Emperor Augustus, another Colonna stronghold. Accused in his last days of monstrous sorcery by his Colonna adversaries, Cola's body could only be disposed of by non-Christians. The tribune had been born in Regola where the majority of Rome's Jews were settled, and they had initially supported the revolution.

Freedom

Goffredo Parise

One day in spring a young American painter named Tom
Corey was pedalling a canary yellow racing bike 'as fast as
the wind' beneath the tall pines of the Villa Borghese park
in Rome. The sky (naturally) was blue, though more light
blue than azure, with clouds, and at the centre of the
clouds was just a tinge of grey and inside the tinge of
grey a powder-puff pink. Tom (naturally too) was wearing
trainers, blue jeans, and a plum red wind-filled glossy silk
shirt hand-painted with big fleshy navy-blue flowers,
bought for a dollar in a Chinese rag store on 42nd Street
in New York. He was blond and blue-eyed, spare and not
overly tall, with the build of a dancer. He pedalled like a
boy, with pep, and was already bright red in the face and

perspiring a bit, so emanating a smell like risen dough just waiting to go in the oven.

As he sped along he passed through some rather gloomy stretches shaded by some sort of dank and dark vegetation with tufa peeping through, and moss too, and these patches cooled him down a bit after the breezy but scorching sunlight which beat straight in his face along the open stretches. He laughed to himself, or grinned, baring fine white doglike teeth with sudden glints of saliva and light, and every so often he narrowed his eyes and cut down his 'rocket' speed, even stopped altogether, and still with eyes half-closed studied intently: a statue, a fountain, a meadow under the umbrella pines, the light filtering through and the different hues of green, from pea green to grey, in the grass below.

He halted for some time beside the so-called house of Raphael, in two minds, with the toe of one shoe on the ground, tense and motionless with eyes narrowing more and more and chewing his little moustache; then he resumed his ride, though more meditatively now, coasting downhill alongside Piazza di Siena, the riding enclosure. His glance swept the shady arena, he braked, leaned the yellow bicycle against a hedge (the bike sinking into greenish black), took a satchel and a small wooden box from behind the saddle, and with these schoolboy items under his arm and in one hand walked on a few paces until he was looking down over the whole wide bowl. Here he sat down on the wall, propped the satchel beside him, took out a sheet of yellow butcher-shop paper which he spread over the satchel fastening it with a clip at either end, and opened the box of pastels, all worn down to little pieces.

No need to add that Tom, like everyone else good-looking and young, and who belongs to a large and wealthy family or a large and wealthy country, was poor but happy. Like everyone who is happy he was scarcely aware he was poor and had no notion he was happy. He ate once a day, more or less, slept in a dump in the Suburra* surrounded by old Roman walls oozing blood and death (though, quite properly, he took blood and death for history) and come evening often danced boogie and rock 'n' roll with certain Negro girls from New York (fashion models), emanating that bready smell and treating them as pure rhythmic material, and they were glad enough to be treated as such.

He spoke a few words of Italian, a very few, and with a sort of wide-eyed miaowing grace to make up for his lack of vocabulary. He was a painter of landscapes and interiors, and every day with his canary yellow bicycle went round Rome or into historic buildings with his tiny

---

* The most notorious plebeian quarter of ancient Rome, still recalled in the name of a piazza in the Monti district of inner Rome.

chalks: he'd stay there an hour, even two if the light didn't alter too much, but if the light changed and it was no longer as happy or as unhappy as his happiness required he'd leave after a quarter of an hour, coming back next day when the sun was high overhead or low down.

He enjoyed finding the colours for things which do not last, most of all those moments of unhappy light in the early morning when the sun is still feeling its way, hasn't yet warmed the walls and the trees and the grass, and everything is still shrouded in something diurnal which nonetheless belongs more to the night than the day. That total absence of direct light, or at most a darting or glancing light, endured such a short while, and this explains why he never stayed anywhere for long. At those times not just the yellow butcher-shop paper on which he scratched his chalks absorbed the damp and the chill but also his skin and his muscles, and all this produced a reciprocal flow between the paper and his muscles and his muscles and the paper.

That spring day and the place he had chosen were one of these times. Tom worked swiftly, frowning a little short-sightedly and lifting his eyes to wait for one of those white-grey-pink clouds to pass over the sun. Since the clouds were racing this would happen soon enough and then Tom would work more swiftly with his little chalks, lowering his eyes close to the paper.

A short way off seated on a small folding chair was a woman who was not old but very nearly old, with her legs swathed in thick greyish pink elastic stockings, and near the woman two young men were leaning against a dark blue car smoking without exchanging a word. One of them had a revolver tucked in his belt.

The woman watched Tom as he drew, eyeing him once in a while and then more and more often with considerable curiosity and that guileless lack of discretion common to old people and children. All the while she was thinking about certain Italian political events of which she had been not only the protagonist (she happened to be a senator) but also witness. The woman's body was strong and sturdy like her bandaged legs but not fat, like that of a peasant woman, and she resembled a very well-groomed peasant woman in the way she dressed and also the way her hair was done. Her face too was that of a peasant but unlike the kind of peasant woman she herself must once have been her face was clouded by something, something that must have happened not long ago, something high-principled and cruel which one notices in the faces of elderly nuns in positions of authority.

All the same the woman observed Tom as though in his movements and his very being and in the way he rubbed the little chalks against the paper he possessed or manifested something she did not recognize, had never seen in her life. She got up very slowly from the little folding chair, taking with her a slim black cane with a curved handle on which she leaned her weight. Her feet were large, stumpy, and unsteady inside black shoes which looked expressly made for them; she advanced on Tom and from close to first stared hard at him and then at what he was doing. For an instant Tom was distracted by a sparrow which alighted on a corner of the satchel, opening and shutting its wings like a tiny umbrella, and the woman seized this moment to say, in Italian: 'I'm not disturbing you?'

Tom gave a little start, looked round at the woman and in that sort of mewing way of his, laughing, and spreading his arms and his hands and fingers in a nervous and shy welcoming gesture as though he wanted to hug her, and reddening as well, said:

'Oh no, *prego*.' He paused a moment and then again said '*prego*'.

'You are an artist, a painter,' said the woman, and her voice was surprisingly beautiful, slightly masculine.

'*Sì*', said Tom and blushed again.

'A foreign painter?'

'*Americano*,' said Tom.

'Ah, American,' echoed the woman, and she slightly inclined her head in a kindly and almost respectful way. There followed a pause in which Tom didn't know what to say with the woman still standing there, unable on the spur of the moment to find any words in Italian to add something to the conversation which had barely begun. The woman, though, forcing her slow and authoritative voice to sound as kindly as possible, said '*Buongiorno*' and went back towards the blue car. The two young men helped her inside and the car slowly drove away.

Months passed, Tom did not see the woman with bandaged legs again and completely forgot her, but not so the woman herself who once in a while when driving by with her two bodyguards on her outings in Villa Borghese caught sight of him through the window. She would give the order to slow down, gaze out a moment, and then the car would drive on silently towards the Senate. Despite her illness and her age the woman was still considered a fighter; not so much as at one time yet she remained, as often happens in Italy, a figure of considerable political prestige. Tom did not know this and very likely never would, Italian political life being so far removed from his own.

But the woman remembered Tom and the memory was always bound up with something that had attracted her in an almost scandalous fashion, she felt, though unfortunately impossible to divine, so much so that she often used to ask herself what it was without ever finding an answer. Several years later an interviewer came to her rescue, a journalist from a woman's monthly who among a great many more put the following question to her: 'Senator, how would you define freedom? Rosa Luxemburg...'

'I know, I know...' the woman interrupted her, and she smiled 'politically' and slightly raised her hand. The smile vanished, her voice became slightly masculine again.

'Freedom is sociali–' and here she broke off an instant. 'Freedom is an American painter in Villa Borghese' had been on the tip of her tongue. She finished her sentence: '...socialism, our socialism.'

Blue Car

Melania Mazzucco

Form IIIC lined up higgledy-piggledy behind the young woman waving a small red umbrella at the blue sky. The PE teacher, sweating nervously, counted the pupils hoping to hell none had got lost, since the coach had set them down a long way from the entrance to the Vatican Museums. Twenty-three, he called out. Form IIIC was all present and correct. The guide started explaining some-thing—perhaps the reason for the almighty queue, or why it was they happened to be standing in that particular spot. But her voice was swamped by the din of traffic, and in any case the pupils were not attending to her: bent over their mobiles, they were all texting their mums, pals elsewhere, or friends further up the line. Ciao-Ciao watched her face, feigning attention and nodding his head—though only from pity. She found such passion for Italian art touching in a little boy from another culture, almost another world. It was only when, an hour later, they were mustered in front of a picture by Raphael—a great Renaissance painter, as the guide took pains to explain—that the maths teacher informed the PE teacher two pupils were missing. He shrugged, whispering back that most likely they'd only gone off to the toilet. He wasn't going to get stressed out for nothing. The guide endeavoured to win over the children by emphasizing Raphael's importance to world art, mentioning also that the poor man died young from a venereal disease. She was counting on their youthful solidarity, but instead Form IIIC was gripped by irrepressible mirth, because the picture in question depicted a naked woman. And the sight, so unexceptional, seemed to these twelve-year-olds ignorant of female anatomy cause for huge embarrassment, generating uncontrollable giggles. So who's missing? the PE teacher asked, cursing the day he'd agreed to accompany the class on this school trip to Rome. Dennis, universally known as Pecora, that is Sheep, on account of his curly fair hair, the other being the little Chinese mute, the boy who never spoke since he didn't understand a thing, and who right from his very first day at school had been dubbed by all Ciao-Ciao because of his unpronounceable name.

Pecora and Ciao-Ciao had not intended to cause a panic. It was just that they'd got bored standing in line, and fifteen-year-old Pecora, the teachers' nightmare who since he failed every exam never went up a class and roosted there like a bird of passage waiting to fly away at the first hint of fair weather, felt cheesed off at the thought of having to traipse round a museum. I didn't come to Rome to see a museum, he said to the other boy, who was gazing up in wonderment at the high walls of the Vatican. Ciao-Ciao nodded. I want to see the house in Big Brother, he went on. Ciao nodded. It's in Cinecittà—how about it? asked Sheep, though it was more like an answer than a question. Ciao nodded. He had only been seven months in Italy. His mother, a worker in a sanitary towel factory, had put him in the school straightaway. Ciao had never uttered a word to anyone. He sat quietly all alone at his desk at the back of the class, behind the disruptive Pecora. The teachers adored his shyness and nice manners. He finds the language a problem, they all agreed, but he'll learn fast, and next year he'll lick the lot of them.

The two boys slipped away unnoticed and soon found themselves in an immense space which Pecora recognized as St Peter's Square from having seen it on television. This is where the pope died, he said to Ciao. The Chinese boy nodded. Pecora asked around where Cinecittà was, but no one knew because they were tourists. Finally they went over to some white cars massed together at the edge of the square. Each was a stunning bridal white. On their roofs they said TAXI. Ciao went closer, placed his hands on a rolled-down window and peered inside. All the cars had meters with numbers in red. The drivers knew where Cinecittà was, but Pecora didn't have enough for the fare. They told them to take the metro. The metro, though, was nowhere to be seen. Yellow buses came by with all their passengers riding up top, out in the sun. Red buses came by: same arrangement. They didn't get on because the driver said the ticket was sixteen euros, these were tourist buses. Green buses came by, full to bursting, with no room for more. Cars huffed and puffed at the traffic lights, stuck in a jam. Never in his life had Pecora seen so many cars, but he didn't want to admit it and let the Chinese boy know this was the first time he'd been in such a big city. Five fabulous dark blue cars whizzed by, negotiating the gridlock by crossing into the emergency lane. They were brand new, enormous. With darkened windows. Ciao gazed after them. Sitting in the back seat of one of them he'd managed to spot a fat man in a tie. Even his suit was the same dark blue. A little pale green bus pulled up, making no sound at all, as though fitted with a silencer. They got in. The driver said they should get off at Piazza di Spagna. That was where they'd find the metro. Cinecittà was the second to last stop on the line, they couldn't go wrong. Pecora announced he was going to get his picture taken right in front of the door to the House. The bus skirted a square with a big column in the centre. Beyond the square, a good way off, something shimmered dark blue. Ciao stuck his head out of the window. Scores of cars identical to the one in which he'd seen the fat old man in blue were drawn up in the sunshine. All that deep blue paintwork was like the sky at night the instant before the stars come out. They were stupendous. You're not exactly great company, pal, sighed Pecora, regretting he'd brought along the Chinese boy instead of for instance the loyal De Paolis who had the desk next to his own. But do you ever watch Big Brother? he asked. The Chinese boy nodded.

In Piazza di Spagna the Chinese boy lingered to look up at the palm trees—incredibly tall and skinny, with little green bunches of hair on top ruffled by the breeze. Pecora's mobile trilled. It was the PE teacher. Pecora didn't answer, just switched off. The sun was shining. All over the huge staircase sat loads of kids, half of them smoking, and Pecora went up to some to cadge a cigarette. The girls summed him up in a trice. Pecora was fair-haired, he had the right cap, the right shoes, the right pants. They didn't even notice the silent little Chinese boy. Five minutes later Pecora and the three girls were disappearing down the tunnel to the metro. Only when he was

on the escalator did Pecora realize he'd lost Ciao. He felt
a bit bad about it. But it was too late to go back and
look for him.

Ciao crossed the square. The shops were all open and
their windows flashed in the sun. There were a couple of
open carriages there, with muscular chestnut horses rooting together in the same sack of oats. He lost his bearings
in the side streets, but just when his feet were beginning to
feel sore he managed to spot the square with the column,
and down there at the far end he sighted the shiny blue
cars.* He set off, heart pounding. But when he reached the
sort of open-air car park he found he wasn't even going to
be able to touch them. There was a metal barrier. Ciao
propped his elbows on the rail. Young men in dark blue
stood by the cars. They were handsome, and strong as
warriors. Ciao stayed there in the sunshine watching all
the toing and froing between the big building that was
there and the blue cars. Mostly elderly men in dark blue
suits got into the cars. The warriors, he soon decided, were
the Emperor's soldiers. Ciao would have given anything to
sit inside one of those cars. After a while he realized the
barrier was mobile. A gentle push opened a gap between
two barriers wide enough for him to slip through, supple
as a cat. The warriors were absorbed in animated

---

* Beyond Piazza Colonna lies Piazza Montecitorio, a restricted zone in front
of the Chamber of Deputies.

conversation, chatting away cheerfully with their backs to him. The cars stood unguarded. Ciao chose the biggest and shiniest, the best. When he got in he was careful not to close the door fully behind him, so as not to make a sound. He sat in the back seat, the one for the Emperor, and it was like sinking into a warm embrace. He fingered the seats in front, they were in pale leather. The dashboard was in dark wood. On the front seat was a bunch of flowers of the most unbelievable red. The car had dark windows. It was like wearing sunglasses. From behind the glasses Rome was even more beautiful. The colours were all much more intense, brighter and sharper. The marble column back there had turned the whitest white. The warriors' suits looked almost ink blue. Ciao decided he was never going to leave that car.

Who the fuck are you? demanded one of the blue warriors suddenly. The voice made him jump. How'd you get in here? What are you thinking of? Are you out of your mind? Out, now! Ciao did not budge. He nodded, smiling. He was so happy he could have burst into tears. The warrior grabbed him by an arm and yanked him out of the car. Ciao was so light he came away as easily as a feather. Next to the blue warrior stood another man also dressed in dark blue—with a white beard and glasses. The car was his. Why, he's just a little boy!—exclaimed the old man. Seeing how small the Chinese boy was, the warrior calmed down too. So sorry, he said to the old man, I don't know how it could have happened, it won't happen again. So what are you doing here?—the old man asked him. Ciao, paralysed with misery, nodded. He doesn't understand, said the young man to two men dressed in a different blue, a sugar-paper blue, who came up. They had pistols in white holsters. They were policemen. He must have got lost, said the old man, while the younger one opened the door of the blue car for him. Lost?— laughed the younger man,—whoever gets lost and climbs aboard a minister's car? Ciao ran his hand over the gleaming bodywork. Beautiful, eh?—said the young man. Ciao nodded. Fancy one of your own?—joked one of the policemen with the pistol in a white holster. Yes, said Ciao. Then you'll have to go into the police force, said the young man. Ciao smiled. No, he said in flawless Italian, I'm going into parliament.

Via Veneto Notes

Ennio Flaiano

June 1958

Together with Fellini and Tullio Pinelli * I'm dusting down one of our old ideas for a film, the one about the young provincial who comes to Rome to make it as a journalist. Fellini wants to update it to how things are today, paint a portrait of this 'café society' cavorting amid eroticism, alienation, boredom, and sudden general prosperity. It's a society which with the passing of the Cold War scare,

---

* Federico Fellini, the film director, and Tullio Pinelli, Flaiano's co-writer on *La dolce vita*. All other figures mentioned are writers or artists. Vincenzo Cardarelli (1887–1959), from Tarquinia, was one of the leading poets of his generation. Giacomo Leopardi, mentioned near the end, was Italy's greatest poet of the Romantic era.

and perhaps as a direct reaction, flourishes more or less everywhere now. But here in Rome owing to the mix of sacred and profane, old and new, the massive arrival of foreigners, the cinema, it wears a more aggressive face, almost subtropical. The title of the film will be *La dolce vita* and we haven't yet written a line; we vaguely take notes and go all over to refresh our memory of certain places. In recent times Rome has got bigger, nastier, richer. Scandals break with the violence of summer storms, people live outdoors, eyeing up and copying each other, filling up the restaurants, the cinemas, the streets, leaving their cars in the very squares which not so long ago enchanted us with their architectural splendour and now look like garages.

One of our locations has perforce to be Via Veneto, where the party atmosphere is ever more hectic; and tonight I intentionally took a walk there, trying to see it lucidly. How it's changed since 1950 when I used to arrive on foot every morning through the Villa Borghese and passed the time of day in Rossetti's bookshop, with Napolitano, Bartoli, Saffi, Brancati, Maccari, and the poet Cardarelli. The air was clean, the traffic calm (Brancati rode a bike), from the baker's wafted a smell of warm brioches, there was a cheerful village bustle to it all, journalists and writers shared aperitifs, the painters had no dealers, hardly anyone flew.

How a street can change! Now summer is on its way anyone can see it's no longer a street but a beach. The cafés spilling onto the pavements—how many now, six, seven?—feature different sorts of sunshade at their tables, just like the bathing establishments in Ostia; and they are not plain street sunshades but fit for a garden party. Some have straw fringes and festoons like on the Hawaiian Islands, others call to mind the era of Offenbach's *La Vie parisienne*, the Great Exhibition, the march of progress, and every table sports miniature flags of all the countries invited to the party.

Cars crawl by like stage gondolas, in jerks, and the public takes the air undulating back and forth with the indolence of seaweed and the bogus assurance of an opera chorus.

So our destiny still lies on the sea.* We're so enamoured of the idea that we've adapted it in the only way consistent with our laziness, turning streets into seaside resorts, devising seaside styles for our houses, our cars, our clothes, and finally for our citizens who look like—and are, deep down—just bathers.

Even conversation is of the beach variety, crude and jokey, with no interest in anything beyond the gastro-sexual. Not long and we'll all be splashing each other and playing ball.

---

* An ironic application of one of Benito Mussolini's most celebrated catch-phrases.

December 1961

Nowadays you can hardly get to Via Veneto; and it's pointless anyhow, it's like a different city. There's no space to park a car within a mile. I walk over, counting four Christmas trees on the way. The festive greetings are all in English. Snow, which when it falls here immobilizes the city for a week, is evoked by tufts of cotton wool on the shop window displays. Metre-high soft toys in the bars and pastry-shops: American anthropomorphism is catching on with the middle classes, what with its man-friendly animals that even resemble humans: billy goats, deer, aproned mice, cat sheriffs, dwarves. Coming out of the tobacconist's I'm struck by a bizarre sight. A girl is standing outside the Café de Paris and on her head she has concocted a hat in the shape of a Christmas tree: by touching a switch hidden in her pocket she makes the coloured bulbs go on and off. Poor girl, she looks sulky, let down, like those little ones at children's fancy dress parties who suddenly dissolve in tears. And the photographers encamped night and day outside the café view her with a mixture of pity and irritation. Perhaps if some famous actor, maybe even Fellini himself, happened to drop by, something might be contrived to put her out of her misery? 'I dunno,' one of the photographers says, 'I suppose if someone gave her a slap . . . If it's not dramatic no one wants the picture.'

This girl has crossed the ocean to try to make it as an actress in the land of *La dolce vita,* and here she is flicking her little light bulbs on and off. Why doesn't her gimmick appeal? What does the public want? Nothing?

April 1952

Every morning the poet Cardarelli plants himself in the only armchair in Rossetti's bookshop considerably impeding business with his sallies and even more with his glum silences which unnerve the customers. Rossetti seems not to take it amiss, in fact it amuses him. Yesterday a young woman writer came in and started poking about among a pile of books, making comments that unfailingly betrayed her nervousness, as well as a desire to be noticed by the poet. She picked up the Sansoni edition of Goethe's works and murmured, 'Oh God no, Goethe again, what a bore!' Cardarelli, who seemed to have dropped off to sleep, remarked almost to himself in the ensuing silence: 'Perhaps, Signora, you're muddling him with the Golden Gate' (which is a pastry-shop in the same street). Today, beaming with excitement, another lady came in and asked Rossetti: 'Do you have *Le Diable au corps*? I've seen the film and now I want to read the book too.' And Cardarelli, out of the blue: 'What an intense intellectual life you have, Signora!' Next a young poet dropped by who amid a thousand compliments begged him to recommend him to a certain journal to take his poems. And he handed him one so he could see for himself it was something out of the ordinary. Cardarelli put on his glasses, fishing them out of the depths of his overcoat, and read the poem with furrowed brow as though perusing a telegram. And finally: 'But this stuff is at most good enough for *La fiera letteraria.*' Then recollecting he himself was its editor, he started chuckling silently to himself until his right eye filled up with tears.

July 1959

At a table at Rosati's, during one of those rapid introductions in which one can't follow a thing but still smiles, I met an American lady, dry, tanned, slim, with something coleopteran about her gaze and her green shot-silk dress. This sensation was confirmed when her friend—in that solemn tone which redeems the gossip of certain stories—informed me that every year this lady takes a sex vacation in France and Italy, three months long, with her husband's full agreement. All apparently on instructions from her psychoanalyst. So she selects her men consoled by the thought she's on the road to recovery.

In her handbag she keeps a little camera which she uses to take pictures of her subjects before or after, preferably in the nude. She's documenting herself as best she can. She has built up quite an archive, which no doubt serves to while away the tedium of the winter months when the cure is temporarily suspended. Though personally I think this archive is the tribute she pays to the modern cult which turns every tourist into a photographer bent on gathering evidence of his life (to be sure he lived).

June 1958

A brash society which expresses its cold urge to live more through exhibitionism than truly enjoying life deserves brash photographers. Via Veneto has been invaded by the breed. There will be one in our film, our hero's inseparable companion. Fellini has the character already clear in his head since he knows the model for it: an agency reporter, about whom he tells me a pretty gruesome story. This fellow was sent off to the funeral of a well-known figure who had died in tragic circumstances to snap the tearful widow; but due to some oversight the film got exposed to the light and the photos didn't come out. The head of the agency says to him: 'Suit yourself. In two hours from now bring me the weeping widow, or you're fired and what's more I'll sue you for damages.' So our reporter dashes round to the widow's house and finds her just back from the cemetery, still in mourning dress and wandering from room to room numbed by grief and exhaustion. To cut a long story short, he told the widow if he couldn't get a picture of her in tears he'd lose his job and consequently also the hope of marrying, since he'd just got engaged. The poor widow wanted to chuck him out: imagine how keen she was to play-act for him having only just wept so much for real. So now the photographer goes down on his knees to implore her to be nice and not ruin him, to cry for just a minute, even pretend to!—only long enough for him to take one snap. It worked. The poor widow, once she'd fallen into the trap of pitying the man, had herself photographed sobbing on the matrimonial bed, at her husband's desk, in the drawing room, in the kitchen.

Now we need to give this photographer a suitable name, because the right name is a big help and means the character will 'live'. We can't seem to come up with anything for our photographer until, chancing to open that marvellous little book by George Gissing called *By the Ionian Sea,* we find an imposing name: 'Paparazzo'. Our photographer will be Paparazzo. He'll never know he bears the honourable name of a hotelier in Calabria of whom Gissing speaks with gratitude and admiration. But names have their destiny.

May 1952

It might seem odd that Cardarelli has chosen Via Veneto to live out his last years. If there is one street he can never have liked this is it. In the first years of our friendship he never went further than the Corso, the streets round Piazza del Popolo, the trattorias in Via del Gambero. His boldest evening excursion was to Tito Magri, a Tuscan vintner in Via Capo le Case, and now here he is in Via Veneto, and in the top half at that, near Porta Pinciana among the hordes of grand hotels, the doormen whistling for cabs, the full-time movie extras now growing beards because they're all working in *Quo Vadis*. Today he was sitting out in the sun seemingly approving of everything, like the old emigrant who has made his money and has come back to his home town. The truth is that what little money he can scrape together goes to pay for a room in a pension in this street and a nurse. Yet he still considers himself rich. As for his love for his actual home town he has exhausted it in his books and there can't be much left over. He knows this is his last port of call.

There is something calculating about his choice, a kind of challenge to the rules of the game which decree an old elephant should go off and hide somewhere far away to die.

September 1958

In three months by the sea we have finished writing *La dolce vita,* and now the usual troubles begin. The producer flatly refuses to make the movie. He gave the script to four or five critics to read and now they gaze upon us pityingly and shake their heads: the story doesn't hang together, it's false, pessimistic, flippant: instead what the public wants is a bit of hope.

On my way home through Via Veneto just before midnight I spot Cardarelli all by himself, sitting at the last table in the Caffè Strega. 'They didn't come to get me,' he says. He's like a tripper who has lost his friends and missed the bus home. The concierge who has the job of helping him up to his quarters around eight o'clock must have forgotten about him. Indeed he turns up soon after and performs a little pantomime of surprise: 'Oh no! Still here? I thought . . .' They make their way through the front door slowly, tottering and teetering, like two revellers sapped by the fun they've had.

Sometimes I feel there's a connection between Cardarelli and the hero of our rejected script. A connection which goes only so far, however. Cardarelli similarly came to Rome from his home town young and penniless to make it as a journalist. When in confidential mood, he used to talk about his first steps in turn-of-the-century Rome as a reporter for *Avanti*. He wrote about everything, doggedly. He was particularly intrigued by the crimes, the ritual mutilations, the love tragedies. He signed himself Simonetto, Calandrino, Caliban! Then illness strikes, followed by long confinement in the same hospital ward in which his father died. His youthful frenzy evaporates, he becomes another person, looks inside himself and discovers poetry, makes it his *raison d'être*, and starts out as a writer all over again. His first prose pieces are already perfect. Rereading them today, with some circumspection and perhaps in the subconscious hope of finding they've aged, I realize that if there's an old man round here it's not him.

June 1962

Via Veneto ever more unrecognizable now, wrecked by its own fame, left to the tourists, easy pick-ups, and the cinema. The 'intellectuals' have followed the painters to Piazza del Popolo, topographically well defended against the assaults of fashion by its wide open spaces, the lack of big hotels in the vicinity, the relatively few cafés. They don't come to Via Veneto of an evening anymore but in the afternoon for the book launches, and not always then. The latest books, three or four a week, are promoted at the Open Gate or the Einaudi bookshop. Everyone's writing. Those not writing are gathering material. If the cultural miracle carries on we'll end up with one writer for every hundred inhabitants.

July 1957

I made a long detour to avoid Cardarelli. I was in a hurry and committed this little act of cowardice, but other friends do so too. From eight in the morning Cardarelli comes downstairs from his pension, which is above the Caffè Strega, and sits at the very first table in the same

café, right by his own front door. The waiters are happy
about it because they know he's a great poet and won the
Strega prize in 1948. They'll explain this to any customer
curious to hear about that gentleman sitting out under the
full blast of the sun in his hat and coat. A strange malady
which makes his legs freeze obliges Cardarelli to don his
entire wardrobe every time he goes out and has to abandon the heater in his room to which he is now deeply
attached. So the waiters respect him, and the café proprietor has issued instructions to charge him low prices
which would seem ridiculous to anyone else but do not
register with Cardarelli since he doesn't know the price of
anything and is no doubt convinced they're the same in
the other cafés.

For the whole day Cardarelli sits there at the café,
keeping to a precise timetable: eight to one, one hour's
break for lunch, then back again from two to eight. At
eight he retires to his room, goes to bed and begins his
titanic battles with the insomnia which only abandons
him at dawn.

Today Amerigo Bartoli made me a present of a drawing showing Cardarelli at the café together with the pension concierge, the same who collects him every morning
and helps him back upstairs in the evening. Often the
concierge sits down unobtrusively beside the poet and
like him watches the lively spectacle of passers-by, the

swarms of pretty girls. In Bartoli's drawing Cardarelli and the concierge have accidentally swapped headgear. The concierge wears the poet's Homburg and he has the concierge's cap.

Bartoli and Cardarelli's friendship goes back a long way, they love each other, but with no holds barred. Bartoli, for instance, refers to Cardarelli as 'the greatest dying poet'. Days later a lady from out of town comes over to greet Cardarelli and says: 'And Bartoli? What's Bartoli up to?' Pulling a heartbroken face, the poet replies: 'He's not growing, Signora, he's not growing!' And still alluding to the painter's small stature adds: 'He can't sleep at night and walks nervously up and down under the bed.'

Nonetheless Cardarelli is ever on the lookout for Bartoli's arrival, and gets frantic if he's late, but the moment he sees him rounding the corner of Via Sardegna he turns his head the other way like a lover who has resolved to break things off, pretending he hasn't seen him.

November 1958

'Oh how nice to feel super-intelligent, get all gooey about sex, be to woman indifferent... Answer every survey, sign any petition, have big opinions to purvey, be a man with a mission... Oh how nice not to be out with what's in fashion, make mass culture your special passion... Swear by art *engagé*, insist industry is hot, and end a perfect day with a revolver shot...'

We were chanting this stuff to ourselves, I and Fellini, as we drove down Via Veneto, when a policeman blew a blast on his whistle and pulled us over. We had shot the lights: three thousand lire fine. 'I haven't a penny on me,' said Fellini, 'but I can write you a cheque.' The policeman eyed us sternly. 'Wait a moment,' Fellini went on, 'I seem to know you. Let's do it this way. You lend us five thousand, we pay the fine, and tomorrow at this same time we'll come here and give you back your five thousand.' Seeing the policeman looked nonplussed, Fellini repeated the proposition: 'How can you lose? If we pay the fine you'll look good with your superiors and we'll be able to get a bit of petrol. If you refuse what happens instead? We don't pay.' 'I don't have five thousand lire,' says the policeman. 'You're having us on. Are you telling me you haven't fined anyone else today? Come on, be a good fellow.' The policeman stared at us still shaking his head, then with a sigh said: 'Alright, get going.'

So now although it seems certain his film won't get made Fellini never stops thinking about it and spends his time picking out faces, contacting actors, sending telegrams, getting to know the shady hangers-on of Via Veneto and environs. He wants to depict an unreal Rome, rebuild everything in the studio or leave to reality what little is unreal already: the Trevi Fountain, St Peter's, the Roman countryside.

March 1960

Do we really need another reality? Isn't this rosy Roman reality enough? Certainly it's not easy to live and examine one's actions in a city where the only industry is the cinema. You end up believing life exists for the benefit of the movies, you acquire a photographic eye, you see reality as a pale reflection of the one living and breathing on the screen. The dog bites its tail. And also ends up finding it good.

December 1960

Once in a while I come across someone who more or less obliquely reproaches me for having collaborated, in *La dolce vita,* in portraying Rome as a den of vice. Odd, because I think just the opposite. I'd like to answer these people in the words of my friend Frassineti: 'There is a form of madness which consists in the loss of everything except reason.' In other words: is it my fault if Vice in Rome so soon becomes rational and utilitarian? And if, not being nourished by passion, it becomes solely a hollow fact, a custom, a source of gratification, a fashion?

It seems to me that one of the reasons, perhaps the chief one, which prevents Rome from becoming a city of great vices is its profoundly family-orientated nature, even in corruption. This trait stems from its being an agglomeration of large villages, horrible towards the periphery, all clustered round the ancient nucleus. Villages inhabited by migrants of the first or second generation who have preserved their provincial habits and customs. So in Rome every great 'vice' takes on the form of a leisure pursuit which once the initial curiosity is past grows tedious. None more picky than the provincial in the matter of vices: not one of them agrees with him, he ends up finding them all ridiculous or expensive, not forgetting they're bad for his health.

The great capitals of Vice base their fame on alcohol, drugs, violence, the grand passions, and above all on Remorse, in other words on the by-products of Sin. Now in Rome no one drinks outside mealtimes. To run across a drunk in the streets at night is increasingly unlikely. You'll see one or two in bars in the suburbs. But there he is, not shouting, not threatening, not thrown out like a sack of potatoes: he's arguing heatedly about football surrounded by sardonic youths who kill a long evening this way. In bars in the centre, like these in Via Veneto, the hard drinkers are as we know probably no more than a hundred, and over time they become objects of admiration, because they're surely much travelled, familiar with the ways of the rest of Europe. Rather than vice-ridden they feel privileged, they enjoy the barmen's respect and any query relating to alcohol and the ways of the beau monde is deferred to their judgement. The rest of the customers drink coffee, orangeade, even milk. For many their indecisiveness when ordering reaches fever pitch until they manage to blurt out to the waiter, with a deep sigh of relief which betrays an equally deep absence of vices: 'A coffee with . . . with just a little drop of milk.' And when the waiter's turning away they summon him back to say: 'Cold milk, mind!' Now, these people are not abstemious because they have decided to combat the forces of Evil or haven't the money: they are abstemious because they have nothing they need to forget and wish to remain lucid, rational—indulge in vice for sure, but with eyes wide open.

There's prostitution of course, but the traits which this activity has come to assume are now so wearisomely hypocritical that in the end it's work like any other, the sole source of funds for certain families, a boost to tourism, small-time business, hire-purchase sales, security for old age, and employment for the pimps. It's of more interest to the economist than the moralist.

So there we have it, a placid panorama dominated by the dictates of reason. The one big attraction remains Sex which, par excellence, means Woman. But the Roman's penchant for Woman never boils over into all-consuming vice and passion. Sex is a comfort, itself practically a family affair. Last summer Lily Niagara came to Rome for some striptease shows. After four days, the establishment where she worked was offering a reduction to anyone paying national insurance.

April 1959

When invited to an official function, Cardarelli gets the waiter at the Caffè Strega to lend him his dinner jacket. His latest outing was yesterday, 25 April, an invitation to a banquet at Villa Madama in honour of a writer who had won the Golden Pen award. Recently Cardarelli also received a prize, the Torre, which is awarded fairly often and more or less to everyone, in a trattoria near the Campidoglio. When presented with the silver tower he was delighted, but next day was much put out when he saw the concierge who'd been despatched to sell that kilo of silver coming back with it. It wasn't silver.

I escorted Cardarelli up to his room. The stench was unbearable, I opened the window which looks onto one of those internal courtyards which are deep and dank and gloomy, inhabited by cats and with a washtub. Viewed from here Via Veneto is just a façade. As soon as you enter these old houses the old Rome of narrow street doors, dark staircases, yards reeking of cabbage and mould grabs you by the throat. Once, until around the end of the last century, here were the gardens of the Ludovisi and

Boncompagni, tree-lined avenues, vineyards, bosky groves graced with statues. The town-planning department didn't care for such stuff (and still doesn't) so it decreed that Via Veneto (then called Via dei Cappuccini) should become the main street of a popular housing quarter. The quarter for the wealthy bourgeoisie, the top state functionaries, the Piedmontese conquerors, was instead to be the Esquiline Hill. So over there they put up Piazza Vittorio Emmanuele with its porticos just like Turin, and giant apartment blocks, balconies, caryatids. Via dei Cappuccini got the basic housing. Then with time, as in a quadrille, rich and poor changed places: the poor moved into the rich people's houses and Via Veneto became the fashionable street. It filled up with hotels, cafés . . . But this courtyard brings home how everything got off to a bad start. The poet's room is tiny, with washing and toilet facilities carved out of one corner. The table is littered with books and papers. 'I've nothing left,' says Cardarelli with just a hint of satisfaction. I see just two photographs, groups of friends from his far-off youth. The heater is next to the window. Cardarelli sits on the bed with his overcoat still on like an emigrant waiting for the ship to leave, or an earthquake victim who seated on his last remaining stick of furniture establishes possession and will not budge for fear of seeing it carted away.

June 1962

I am reading Sandro De Feo's *Gli inganni* [The Deceptions]. The story takes place in Rome on a single day. Perhaps owing to something rather urgent and breathless about the narration, it feels like a gust of wind whirling away particles of dust, leaves, old scraps of paper, and also some kind of imponderable and precious material, our very own lives, the futile delusions, the labour of years, our love for a city which is unique and blithely lets itself be loved and loathed, in accordance with the moods and spectacles it offers. The real Rome lies in shadow, reveals itself only as the years pass, and becomes a landscape of memory, a part of ourselves: the most secret and sole part from which some sort of salvation may come for us. The other Rome may infuriate but betrays its desire to please far too easily to become truly dangerous. You end up laughing at it. For instance De Feo says of Via Veneto: 'So tonight it's Via Veneto. The spectacle of the flesh market under the green awning is nothing but what it is, and yet assuredly my wind-flayed nerves make me exaggerate its obscenity and grotesquerie. If I had the energy to do anything at all I'd burst out laughing, like when I read the tales of the Marquis de Sade at moments when the author lays it on too thick...'

The green awning... I forgot about that newfangledness. In the Via Veneto the sunshades have vanished from the café tables, those sunshades that gave it the look of a beach. They have been replaced by long metal awnings covered in fabric or with canopies in some transparent material. As darkness falls, neon lighting comes on beneath the awnings.

June 1959

Yesterday 15 June Cardarelli died in the Polyclinic, where he had spent a month. A great devotee of Leopardi, he died in almost the same way, from ice-cream induced indigestion which then degenerated into bronchial pneumonia. For a month he had stopped speaking altogether; except that once in a while if someone came into his room he'd mutter under his breath: 'What bores!'

Fellini is at last shooting *La dolce vita* at Cinecittà. He has had a slice of Via Veneto rebuilt in the studio, not the corner where the poet lived but the more recent and more crowded one by the Café de Paris. Faced with that implacable reconstruction I felt like laughing out loud and next moment was seized by a gut-wrenching melancholy. In the projection room I saw some rushes of the film. The baroque excess with which Fellini amplifies that world of Via Veneto brings to mind a waxwork museum, the lurid imaginings of Lenten preachers when they describe flesh corrupting and putrefying. It reminds me of those gigantic paintings by Valdes Leal in the Charity Hospital in

Seville, where above the corpses of bishops float scrolls saying things like *Finis gloriae mundi*: Thus ends all worldly glory. Fellini as hellfire preacher? An intriguing notion. 'Perhaps I should have put Cardarelli in some corner, like a kind of brooding premonition.' 'He died yesterday,' I say. 'Yeah, see what I mean?'

Lorette Ellerup

Francesco Mandica

So Jonas and Lorette left for Rome.

The tickets were a present from their son Asmus, something like a reparation, or an anniversary.

In the plane they appeared to be a completely normal couple: few words passed between them, and these muted by their fear of flying, almost whispered. Denmark seen from a height made a queer impression on Jonas, like an old woman's enormous foot contorted with arthritis. Lorette alternated her reading between the SAS in-flight magazine, the guidebook, and bits she'd cut out from a *National Geographic* insert on the Baroque in Rome. She was on her way back to Rome, where forty years earlier she had been the recipient of a Royal Academy scholarship. Back to Rome where she had experienced turbulent love affairs, wild remonstrations, the clack of her high heels on the wide flight of steps coming down from the Quirinal Palace towards the Trevi Fountain. The sentries outside the presidential palace stock-still at four in the morning. Back to Rome with that old desire—still not quite extinguished despite her years—to be an artist, to cut a dash at private viewings, radiating a beauty which was already waning at twenty.

At sixty, Lorette had a heavy bosom, ballooning only at the base as though conforming to the pull of gravity, suspended well down her front, remote from the breastbone. An inverted Y. But really all her body seemed intent on spontaneous collapse: over time, even her eyes had come to resemble minuscule commas, and as though by natural prolongation the concentric bags at their extremities similarly sagged towards the ground. And had she not kept it permanently up, her hair too would have much preferred descent. Her hands were long but not tapering, rigid if anything: roots straining down to resume their original function. And planted on those two slender legs of hers, her body had lost all its former agreeable distinction, its centre of gravity having slipped a couple of inches below the tip of the nose, earthwards again. Lorette Ellerup always looked like she was hunting for something at her feet. Particularly when walking.

For certain very good reasons Lorette had chosen interior design for a career, a profession which after all had some pretensions to art. Also it permitted her to maintain that odd posture, feigning close attention to detail while perusing potential purchases. The sheen of a fabric, a perfectly hung engraving unhooked for her scrutiny, prodding sofas and armchairs: all things her biological prostration could easily handle.

But interior design meant above all getting to know women. Women who made her hormones run riot. Because Lorette had married a man but loved women. Back to Rome, then, the presidential guards stock-still and appalled, for it was right there that Lorette brought her lovers, to that corner where the Quirinal Palace resembles a bastion, but so defenceless and futile that even wild flowers have conquered it. And kissed them.

Jonas, on the other hand, had never been to Rome. And once they and their baggage were installed in their room in the Hotel Cavour, Jonas wondered why his wife had been so very insistent about coming to Rome. Rome, the very name is so crass and obvious.

This is what he was pondering while propped against the bedhead with the pillow under his bum, irked by the hum of Lorette's depilator. The notion began to grow on him that she had only come here to seek out some old will-o'-the-wisp, some curio from her past. He had long learned to live with this marriage composed of the most humiliating of betrayals, and all in all he had nothing for which to reproach his wife. Who when she was about twenty-five had acted much like wild oranges, which are part orange and part lemon. And bitter. Lorette had picked him for a husband not for the sake of propriety, and not for status, and least of all for love. For plain simple enduring friendship. Loyal friendship, old-fashioned courtesy, bridled affection. Restricted therefore to very private moments of tenderness, deeply meaningful, yet utterly passionless. She had been the one to make the leap to trying out sex, as though to slap a stamp of approval on the relationship as it really stood, legitimize her contention that a convergence of intent without the least physical attraction could guarantee both of them a measure of serenity. Neither felt any pleasure that first time. Nor did it ever happen again. Between them, that is. Lesbians go with lesbians. Husbands with women. That's just how it is.

During her marriage Lorette would take off once in a while, spend periods away with Simon Olsen furnishing houses in Jutland, though more often this was simply what she wanted the other two members of her family to believe. At times she had tried going away for good, beguiled by some forty-year-old. But she wanted her son Asmus for herself, with a maternal impulse nobody would ever have suspected she possessed. So then she would come back home wearing what hopefully the others took to be an air of childish acceptance of defeat, nicely gauged to elicit tenderness without provoking resentment. And on her return she would invariably cook a special Sunday dinner.

Jonas passed at least two of their three days in Rome with his nose in the air, literally, searching for a little bit of sky. He even managed to reconnect with Lorette when, in the Capitoline Museums standing in front of Pietro da Cortona's *Rape of the Sabines*, the two of them exchanged a conspiratorial glance. Because he intuited that the violence depicted in the painting, that abuse, though softened by the beauty of the modelling, was the very same Lorette sensed in men, the same that had made her have a son and love women. Violence all compacted in the loins, a well-oiled pornographic machine, the rapid spasm (which in the painting were pollutions of colour): it was thus he imagined his wife's unease. So a good friend indeed, one who knew her well.

Those two days were spent in secluded places out of the sun, in the cool of marble, apses, courtyards. Rome was not as resplendent as Jonas had imagined and Lorette remembered: it was more a necrosis of rotting plants rooting in fountains, of narrow lanes with high-sounding names leading nowhere, a disjointed maze of piazzas congealed by time, a prolapsus of rubble reconfigured in different shapes. The churches in particular gave them that impression, as though put together from an assemblage of ancient tombstones half-dissolved in plaster. They agreed on this when they had descended into the ossuary of Santa Maria dell'Orazione e Morte, on the Via Giulia where it approaches the bridge.

They ate with relish, trying out everything on the long trolleys of antipasti which tempted them. Yet for all their undeniable fascination, even the trattorias seemed to them darkly forbidding. Presided over by wiry waiters bearing dishes of pasta swimming in milky sauce.

Lorette seemed to him to have shelved any attempt to dig up the past. Apparently fully absorbed in her meal or in deciphering a Latin inscription, she evinced no yen to see the sites of her youth again, nor was she tempted to bring up old haunts and anecdotes with her husband. Theirs was a silence which came close to fulfilment. Albeit in a form hardened by the inescapable nature of their union.

Only the last day was something else. The day before their departure.

Lorette was the first to awake and had already gone for breakfast before Jonas had even managed to haul himself upright by pressing his knuckles into the mattress. She was mysteriously vivacious and on her return presented her husband with a yogurt and an almost too lavish ration of cereal. Holding herself erect with her handbag clutched a little awkwardly against her stomach, she told her husband she intended to go out and buy Asmus certain shoes they had seen together. It looked like a beautiful day, long blue rays filtered into the room. The only detail which struck Jonas as curious was the headscarf Lorette was wearing.

'Why the cravat on your head?' asked Jonas.

'My hair's a bit scruffy.'

They agreed to meet up for lunch by the Chiesa Nuova. After lunch they made their way to the other side of the city, crossing the river at Ponte Sant'Angelo by way of Monte Giordano and Via del Panico. They walked upriver on the opposite bank and entered Trastevere along Via della Lungara. They made a brief right-hand detour, popping into the Botanical Gardens a moment, then carried on as far as Santa Maria in Trastevere before doubling back towards Ponte Sisto, and in the widening next to Piazza Trilussa called at a bar all done out in American-style chrome at the mouth of Vicolo del Cinque. Jonas was ready to drop. Lorette, who had thereby achieved her objective, took leave of him with the excuse of certain gifts she needed to buy at Olsen's behest. Jonas watched her walk away obscured by the wings of the cars whose headlights picked up now some detail of his wife's coat, now that quaint headdress. Lorette walked straight on without losing that slight inclination, heading in the opposite direction to her husband. The insert in the *National Geographic* spoke of the church of San Francesco a Ripa as one of the least touristy places but of considerable artistic merit. Even she had never before seen the Altieri chapel where the blessed Ludovica Albertoni was preserved, 'a late work by Lorenzo Bernini'. She arrived just as the church was about to shut. Not that this was her intention, she later insisted. She had no idea what she was about to see inside.

Tacked on to the far end of the transept, the Altieri chapel was a sort of tunnel at the end of which loomed a massive carpet of stone all undulating in great folds, and on it a woman. A woman of marble, frozen in the act of pressing her hands to her bosom. A saint, a martyr, canonized for her pious devotion. 'The Blessed Ludovica Albertoni, Roman Widow, of the Third Order of St Francis, renowned for her virtue.' A woman stretched out on a divan, sinking into a lace-fringed cushion. Of marble. Suspended above her was the only thing which at that moment might have reminded Lorette she was in church: an altarpiece in which could be made out the Virgin, the infant Jesus, and possibly St Anne. Lorette went up to the base. She saw a frozen woman with head tipped back and slightly thrust towards the onlooker, lips parted a fraction. A woman fondling breasts of stone.

A woman frozen at the moment of orgasm. The tension in her stomach muscles was accentuated by the marble drapery which grew more intricate towards the groin, like a whirlpool. The veil covering her hair hardly gave her the appearance of a nun, it was more like a sheet from which she had broken thrashing out of the embrace, just in time to escape suffocation. Lorette knotted her cravat more firmly under her chin as though to clamp her jaw shut, while glancing round to check no one could see her. She also took off her shoes, slipping one into each side pocket of her coat. With heels uppermost, sticking out from her flanks like handlebars. She wanted to reach her hiding place before the church closed completely. She began to scale the stone carpet, holding on tight to the folds to haul herself up, heels digging in deep despite the slippery hindrance of her nylon tights. She managed to grasp the statue's arm and then clambering onto the dress dug her own fingertips into the gaps between each of the Blessed Ludovica's spread fingers. That way she had her right arm completely free, ready to caress. She put her hand in the prone woman's lap, trying to find a way into the folds of marble to feel inside the whirlpool so she could offer her own contribution to that ecstasy. Her excitement combined with the physical strain compressed her temples, which were pulsing. Her intention was to conceal herself in the hollow between the statue and the frame of the painting above it. Then lie a while there, stretched out as in a coffin alongside that stupendous embalmed creature. But before climbing right over her she wanted to kiss her. Straddling her with both hands pressing down on the statue's plexus, skirt riding above her knees, with one toe still on the stone carpet and the other leg stretching for a foothold, she flung herself forward and, panting with exhaustion, managed to kiss her neck. At the moment her lips touched Ludovica's, the moment heat met cold, the moment Lorette longed to awaken the woman and finally kill the votary, at that moment a priest arrived.

In the instants following all the hullabaloo in the nave, Lorette's saliva along the neck and on the tip of the nose managed to make the statue even more radiant. In those few, brief, luminous moments before the police car arrived. Lorette acted confused, deploying an Italian of not even rudimentary standard.

Jonas and Lorette flew back to Copenhagen next day. Tired though she was, Lorette at once set about preparing a beef stew with redcurrants and sweet potatoes.

Two Days to Christmas

Elisabetta Rasy

Ugly hag, I thought, while endeavouring to put the smokescreen from yet another cigarette between the two of us during that insufferable evening among long-time women friends, wafting it craftily towards her face, at her eyes, at those eyes which had always seemed to me to lack real lustre and now looked truly stagnant in the midst of that detestable gathering under the unreal restaurant lighting which was much too strong yet opaque, blurring everyone's features in the crowded dining room which was now slowly emptying to the great relief of those remaining; because for all that we were well into winter, the December sirocco, as happens in Rome particularly in the narrow streets of the historic centre, induced more than a semblance of the oppressive mugginess of summer.

Ugly hag, I thought with gathering fury, so what's it matter to you who've never been able to stand the sight of me if I happen to smoke too much?

In fact on seeing me light up my fourth cigarette in the after-dinner lull which dragged on listlessly after a lot of strained conversation in which our ancient disagreements and old antipathies had duly resurfaced from the moment eyes first met, or at least right from when we started choosing the antipasti—on seeing me once more huddled over my lighter like a thirsting soul stoops to water or a fugitive tries any door to elude pursuers, Angelica, the supposed friend with whom I'd been expected to spend an evening of fond reminiscences following the conference on the writer Colette, had begun plaguing me with fatuous questions about my smoking.

As always, her general tone of voice and her manner of reasoning were not overtly moralistic but shamelessly self-regarding.

The nub of the matter was ridiculous: at that time in our lives we both smoked around ten cigarettes a day, which is not too bad an average. And having established this common number we might have been satisfied to leave things there had not she with that pig-headedness I knew all too well from university debates on women and literature, and with the identical combination of obtuseness and arrogance, started to insist that the ten cigarettes I smoked were much more damaging to health since they were all crammed into such a short space of time—I had unwisely let on that I only smoked towards the end of the day, anyhow never before mid-afternoon—whereas the ten she smoked, being spread evenly over the entire day, were no harm at all.

It was pointless replying to that, and I didn't, but a feeling of gloomy weariness came over me as I counted the minutes separating us from our final farewells.

No, I told myself, between women there is no such thing as inevitable sisterhood, and above all there need not be: Angelica and I, as I can finally admit after these twenty years, have nothing in common despite our common interests, the common social circles we frequented at a certain point in our lives, our common approach to active campaigning on behalf of women.

We have nothing in common, luckily, I kept repeating to myself, and no one shall ever again be permitted to lump us together.

No one: not zealous deans of faculty in search of female approval, not women heads of department setting up tedious conferences by picking names out of a hat on the basis of foggy hearsay, not local authority bureaucrats etcetera, etcetera . . . No one! At long last, I thought as

I carried on puffing smoke in her face, after years of suspect and spurious solidarity I've found the courage to tell myself how things really stand, and to tell anyone else.

Yet I still felt no better for it, and that drained feeling turned into the oppressive torpor which engulfs us when our hearts are flooded with disappointment.

I picked up the offending objects—cigarette packet and lighter, that is—from the tabletop and felt for my handbag.

Only then did it dawn on me.

When the five of us had got round the table for four—because the one for four was the only table free near the French window which we had all made a beeline for because the heating was turned up so high—Angelica had seated herself comfortably on one of the longer sides with her back to the rest of the dining room, two other friends from our little group had taken the two ends, and Elena and I had sat down together on the other long side with our backs to the half-open French window on the other side of which stood one of those rectangular flower pots you often see in Rome set out on the pavement to prevent cars parking too invasively. I had propped my bag against my chair, down on the floor, not too far from the edge of the French window.

It must have been the irritation I at once feared Angelica's talk and tone would arouse in me that made me so stupidly careless: everyone knows that when eating out in Rome you have to make sure handbags are kept well out of reach of any passing rapacious hands.

And so it must have been the actual intense irritation which true to form her talk and tone provoked in me that made me so distracted as to fail to keep my eye on it during the course of the evening.

No matter, now the bag was gone. And as always happens on these occasions until we accept the evidence of our own eyes, all five of us looked for it under the table, on nearby chairs, and under other tables in a kind of grotesque and pointless pantomime.

By this time my torpor and irritation had turned to desperation: obviously inside my handbag were all the usual essentials for our daily lives—from driving licence to credit card—which have now become nothing less than the artificial organs without which we cannot function as social animals.

But my desperation, I realized, wasn't really about the actual physical loss I'd suffered; it was because from that moment on Angelica had come to embody everything that was false and misguided about my life, all the double standards that bound me to the world, all the conniving compromises which out of laziness, confusion, inertia, I permitted to attach me to extraneous people for whom I felt no genuine attachment at all.

The missing handbag—my alter ego, my sole weapon of self-preservation during all that sultry Roman winter evening caught in the web of a pretentious supper party—at this juncture no longer pointed the finger at Angelica but straight at myself: I who in chasing after ludicrous and illusory idols like that cretin Angelica was constantly mislaying everything, and most of all myself.

By that late hour—it was nearly midnight—the restaurant had become suffocatingly hot, or hot enough at any rate to smother my powers of thought in an extreme malaise and my fellow diners' clumsy efforts to help me in meaningless confusion.

Then suddenly I remembered. I hadn't had it for so very long, so my dealings with it were still somewhat wary and awkward.

Still, there was one thing about it I remembered I'd cottoned on to at once: it's not the person receiving the call who as with old-style landlines is normally the one to say, 'Where are you?' 'Where are you ringing from?' now it's actually the caller who asks the person picking up the phone: 'Where are you?' Because with cellphones or mobiles or whatever you like to call them, what we now want to know the moment the other person says 'Hello' is no longer how they are, as was traditional before, but where they are, so we can picture them in our mind's eye and thus—exactly as before—use the call to pinpoint the person calling and so bring them closer to our hearts.

So I dialled the number, my own number.

I was guided by a flash of inspiration, as well as desperation: whoever took my bag, making the most of my befuddled state brought on by Angelica causing me to fall out with the female half of the species, that is my own gender, is not a professional thief. It can only be one of those roaming insecure creatures of the night who hover about the streets of Rome like fumbling nervous birds of prey and basically pounce only on those who are even more fumbling and nervous than themselves... My bird of prey could not fail to respond to the irresistible decoy of my cellphone cooing its siren call deep in the belly of my handbag.

The ringing tone, the one I could hear with my trembling ear pressed to the receiver of the restaurant's coin-operated phone, went on for quite some time. I knew that at the other end inside the bag was tinkling a stupid tune something like the song of the seven dwarves in *Snow White* when they're coming home from the mine. I let it go on ringing: even if he doesn't want to answer he won't know how to stop it and he'll grab the bait.

And so it was. The voice which after a couple of minutes emitted a feeble 'Who is it?', rather than the croaking of a raptor sounded more like the strangled twitter of a wounded sparrow.

'It's me,' I said, 'the owner of the handbag—give it back and I'll give you all the money in the wallet.'

For some time I heard nothing, then a sound with no distinguishable features—neither male nor female, neither young nor old—asked me with mysterious haste: 'Are you still in the restaurant?'

'And where are you?' I demanded in my turn. There was no immediate reply, and I had the impression the person truly did not know where.

'Listen,' I said then, 'we'll meet up in fifteen minutes, that's on the dot of midnight, under the little elephant in Piazza Minerva—you know it?'

'I know it,' replied the voice almost tripping over itself now, and adding with the same mysterious urgency as before: 'All right then.'

Ten minutes of the quarter-hour I had to reach the piazza, which in any case was not far, were expended in debate with my little group of fellow diners, because while Elena and the other two showed only concern for me, Angelica naturally had to make an issue of principle out of it: the correct response was to turn up all five of us together in a compact female collective, sisterly and resolute in its solidarity against the male individualist—

individualistic even in crime—and certain to use violence against a woman on her own.

That was the moment when finally truly exasperated by the pointless waste of an evening and the sirocco, and vaguely excited by the theft I'd undergone and that small voice whispering into my cellphone, the words which had for so long been festering in my throat at last rose to my lips: Angelica, we are not sisters, I feel no solidarity, and above all we are not friends.

I walked off blissfully into the night picturing her lips pursed in her know-all face composing some appropriate theoretical comment on my madness—as blissfully as if I'd forever liquidated some petulant part of myself, and readying myself for the meeting.

This was not the first time I'd been robbed in the centre of town; once with Ambra we had been subjected to a genuine mini-armed robbery. That time our assailants had been scruffy curly-head kids like any other kids their age. Now there was the risk that the person who stole my handbag was a fairly desperate junkie, maybe with acute withdrawal symptoms.

Yet I was absolutely fearless: I would be calm, decisive, and cold as ice.

Under the obelisk in the famous piazza which was still reasonably animated at that hour, as I had calculated so as not to run too many risks, there was no one to be seen. Or rather no one corresponding to my expectations. In the light shed from the hotel to the right of the church a couple was kissing up against the monument, someone was hurrying towards a car, others were chatting together as they sauntered off in the direction of the Pantheon. Then, next to the pedestal of the monument, by the corner between the front of the church and the building opposite the hotel, I spotted my handbag. I went up to it slowly, and a little further on, crouched in the shadow I saw the thief.

It was not a man at all, but a girl with long blond hair dressed in a thin little floral tunic under a hideously ancient and shapeless padded leather jacket. Tiny, bent, with head cocked like someone having to twist their neck to peer at something towering over them and unable to get to their feet.

I suppose she was about twenty, not much more or not much less. She said nothing, simply gazed at me. I too gazed at her, wondering out of what nest, from what flight she could possibly have tumbled, and trying not to frighten her too much with my searching look. Needless to say, she did not scare me in the least. I would have liked to grill her, get her to tell me why she wandered around in the night doing things that terrified her, as was now quite evident.

But I said nothing, because just as I was about to open my mouth I recollected Angelica's smug self-assurance—a word for everything, a word on everything—and I chose the milder path of silence.

In silence she set the bag beside me. In silence I took it up.

Then in silence we looked at each other a moment.

She didn't ask me for what was in the wallet, and I hesitated to give it her. Not to break our agreement, but because I felt a little bit ashamed to get out the money and hand it over.

Then I did it, and the darkness veiled my movements.

As she was about to take the notes from my hand— perhaps not as much as a hundred thousand lire*—the idiotic jingle commenced playing on the cellphone. We both jumped, as though both of us were the thieves now. Then I smiled at her and she smiled back. She took the money and stayed squatting there peacefully, and I who had been stooped very close to her straightened up, said 'Ciao', and walked away.

I felt in excellent spirits; my gender—the female gender— no longer seemed insufferable like half an hour before, and so that must mean myself too, and I pictured Angelica's fury as she listened to my mobile ringing unanswered in the night:

---

* About sixty euros in today's money.

I was sure she was not in the least bothered about my safety and just wanted to subject me to another lecture on sisterly solidarity.

I looked back to see if I could make out the little thief, but there was nothing on that side of the monument and by now the square was only peopled by shadows.

Then I slipped away into the night, light-footed, calm, in no hurry at all. Tomorrow I could take things easy: in two days it would be Christmas.

Isabella De Luna

Matteo Bandello

Caught off guard, most women have a quick retort to suit
the moment and instantly come out with something appropriate, and seeing this is how nature made them,
obviously the wittiest and best-equipped must be those
who have most experience of society. And what women
have kept company with a greater diversity of brains than
the courtesans at the court of Rome? There all the most
brilliant and cultured talents in the world congregate,
Rome being our universal motherland. There fine writing
of every sort flourishes, in Latin and Greek and the vernacular, and prodigious legal minds, consummate natural
and moral philosophers, and there you'll see painters
performing miracles, sculptors who can cut living faces

from marble, metalworkers able to cast whatever they fancy. In short, there each and every art has reached perfection, to the extent that anyone hoping to excel in any accomplishment should go to Rome to learn it. On the other hand, as wise Ovid says, all too often roses and nettles root in the same soil, and so equally in Rome one finds the best and worst of humankind. Take the courtesans, or rather those who lend an air of respectability to their profession by usurping this name of courtesan. Generally speaking, they are all more greedy for money than flies for honey, and if ever some young lamb falls into their hands I can tell you that unless he is unusually smart and keeps his wits about him, with no need of a razor they'll fleece him on the spot and skin him alive.

Anyone hoping to catalogue everything courtesans get up to wherever they go would in my opinion be biting off more than he can chew, since even if he thought he'd finished there would still be twice as much to say. Among the many in Rome is one named Isabella De Luna, a Spaniard who has wandered half the globe. She went to La Gaulette and Tunis to succour our famished soldiers. For a time she followed the emperor's court through Germany and Flanders and various other places, happy to hire out her mount to whoever fancied a canter. Then not so long ago she quit and went back to Rome, where those who know her say she is the wittiest and sauciest woman who ever lived there. She is highly amusing in any company, even with men from the highest walks of life, for she rubs along with every sort and can give as good as she gets. In fact she is pure delight, affable, intelligent, and lightning quick in her repartee no matter what the topic. She speaks very good Italian, and if anyone tries to needle her don't think she's put off or at a loss for words when it comes to fighting her corner, for she has a biting tongue and bows to no man, lashing back like a cat-o'-nine-tails. In fact she's so brazen and full of herself she boasts she can make anyone she chooses flush with shame and never change colour herself.

Now it happened she owed a merchant a certain sum of money for various items she had obtained from him and kept stringing him along with promises of letting him have tomorrow what was due today, always insinuating he might call it quits for a ride or two. But the merchant, who wanted his money and not a pig in a poke, paid no heed and pressed for satisfaction on his terms. And of course every time it came to settling up she played stone deaf. Seeing how matters stood, and realizing that unless he resorted to other means he would likely never be paid, the merchant called on the governor of Rome, who was Monsignor De Rossi, bishop of Pavia, and after putting his case got him to issue a summons against Isabella instructing her to appear in person on such and such a day before the governor's own tribunal. When the court constable called at Isabella's lodgings he found her outside on the street joking with some of her cronies. He handed her the summons and in the presence of everyone also issued verbal instructions to report at the stated time, as is the custom. Now Isabella, who along with her other memorable traits roundly blasphemes God and every saint in paradise, male and female, took the summons sheet and giving the constable a withering look burst out in fury and indignation: *Pesa a Dios, que quiere esto boracho vigliaco?* Which is as much as to say, In God's name what's he want, this drunken wimp? Next, unable to control her anger, she ripped up the paper and with utter contempt and disrespect, through the back of her skirts as if she had just voided her bowels, right there in front of everyone used the pieces to wipe her hole. Then she disdainfully returned the shreds to the constable, and told him to bugger off.

Scraps in hand, he sped off to present them to the governor's deputy, sparing no detail in recounting Isabella's response and her every action in making a mockery of him. Shocked by such rank temerity and presumption on the part of a shameless prostitute, the deputy reported everything to the governor himself, forcefully arguing that the woman's impudence was beyond the pale, an appalling example of gross contempt for his office which deserved the harshest punishment so that others would learn never to presume to take such liberties in mocking the magistrate's officials and holding his orders of so little account. The governor was indeed in no doubt that the outrage could not be passed over lightly, in fact must be made an example of, but mindful that the delinquent was a woman and a common prostitute, was reluctant to apply as much rigour and severity as the case demanded. All the same, to make sure Isabella's rank temerity did not go unpunished he had her publicly apprehended by the chief of police and conducted to the Tor di Nona jail.

On examination by the judge, who heard her deposition first, she answered in such a way as to make the charge seem a travesty and nothing to do with her, though in the end she did admit to the money she owed the merchant, pleading for a good many months in which to pay it back. But seeing a year had already elapsed since she obtained the goods he sentenced her to pay the amount in full before being released from prison. Faced with how much business would suffer the longer she spent in jail, since she couldn't turn a penny in that place, I don't know how but she managed to pay the merchant. Then, just when she presumed she was free to go home little the worse for wear, the judge sentenced her to fifty good lashes on her bare arse on the public highway. The sentence was posted and so half Rome turned out for such a fine sight on the day it was carried out. A sturdy constable hoisted her onto his back, and in full view the executioner pushed her skirts over her head to make her bare her Colosseum, then with a stout whip so savagely scourged her buttocks that her bum, which at first flashed lily-white, in no time flushed blood red. After this fearsome and humiliating hiding, once her skirts had been lowered and the constable had set her free, she behaved exactly like a mastiff when it gets out of its bed in the straw and gives itself a good shake, then goes its way. She did the same, and despite her smarting buttocks walked off with not the slightest trace of shame on her face, as though making her way home after a couple of wedding parties.

The Rubber Twins

Vincenzo Cerami

She and her brother were two India rubbers, and I had no idea until that moment. Her name was Delfina, his I no longer recall. I used to meet up with them almost every day, or to tell the truth Delfina more than her brother. We'd pass the time pretty superficially, talking about nothing in particular, things instantly forgotten, never going deep. This perfectly natural way of saying everything and nothing got us so accustomed to avoiding anything problematic that we scarcely ever spoke about ourselves, our lives, our work. A quick mention in passing, before getting back to the usual trivialities.

As time went on we got together more often, and I started seeing her mostly on her own. We made love one day after lunch, with no great transports, still chatting about this and that. We'd see a film and afterwards go window-shopping in the smart streets around the Spanish Steps, never with our arms about each other, never holding hands. After all, we'd made no commitments, and our need to be together, even touch, was in no way possessive. Not for a moment did I fear to lose her, in fact I'd generally show up with my thoughts elsewhere. By now we were seeing each other every day, and each time I had the impression months had gone by. I had no idea simple everyday reality could be so agreeable, and with so much to talk about! We floated like water lilies.

And now here I was, staring in amazement, gazing at her and her brother with my eyes popping. Their last name was Buzzi, twins who grew up in Como. We got acquainted at the corner bar near the metro station in Via Lepanto, here in Rome. We'd often pop in around the same time, I for cigarettes, she for a packet of mints, her twin for a coffee with a drop of milk. One morning, laughing, we introduced ourselves. Then some evening we ran into each other in a pizzeria. So we became quite friendly, and I started going with Delfina. They told me they worked together, but to be honest I never properly understood what they did precisely. For a while he dropped out of circulation, giving no reason. I thought he was jealous of his sister, but we two had never made a big deal of it, and that's how it remained. I've always been of the opinion that the most tricky relationships are the ones that for good or ill end up lasting longer than usual. Because you get into the habit and you build up no end of obligations towards this other person who chooses to share her time with you and something of her inner life. And the truth is the affair with Delfina was getting to be another of these somewhat perilous attachments. All the more so because we were so good together, in this free and easy way. At the outset I privately made a big thing of this novel way of existing, conversing, talking about nothing, making love. Up to then I'd sooner or later always end up sobbing on the woman's shoulder, or collecting her tears on mine, but now the days were like one long enchanting sort of promenade, the sun was never too hot, the air forever balmy, and we never thought of bringing an umbrella unless it was raining. So there you have it: I'd fallen head over heels according to the simplest and oldest rules in the book. Nights, after delivering her to her door, I'd carry on babbling away on my own. I even started losing some weight, and just the idea of having to die some day or other, like everyone else, gave me quite a bit of heartache. If I wasn't with her I was dreaming about her, and when I wasn't dreaming about her I couldn't face sleeping.

And yet in Delfina's presence all this torment vanished like a boozy night next morning: a wee headache, a rueful grin. I liked her just as she was and never must she change, not one jot.

And then came the day I finally understood the origin of her unbelievable lightness of being, and her twin brother's extreme, saintly discretion. That's when I resolved to start a new chapter in my life, and now I know it's the last.

I suppose it was about six-thirty in the evening. We'd caught the 280 in Via Cicerone for Monteverde. We stood the whole way, and I loved breathing in the scent of her hair every time the bus braked. She kept peeking at her watch. We got out at the last stop on Viale dei Quattro Venti. This time, for some reason, she asked me in. She and her brother lived on their own in a plain house in wine-red brick right under three enormous high-rises. Just one big empty room. Their twin beds, a cooker, and a little door into the bathroom were all down one end. Her brother was waiting for her wearing a very close-fitting black T-shirt on top of tights, also black, wringing his hands because Delfina had turned up late. She pulled a swift solemn face, checked her watch one last time, and dashed to the bathroom to change. I didn't say a word, seating myself on a little bench away from the light and eyeing the lad, who didn't once condescend to look at me. I watched him limber up, giving his muscles a rub down then bouncing about on his toes. Delfina came out of the bathroom dressed the same, in black tights, and got straight on with some breathing and stretching routines. After a while the Buzzi twins turned to face each other, holding each other's gaze for a long time. And then their exercises began.

As I say, I stared in utter amazement: they were two India rubbers, two creatures with apparently not a bone between them, so elastic they could turn their bodies into a ball of string or a spiral or a baroque hieroglyph. She tapped her crotch with her forehead, he stroked his behind with the back of his neck. Then, propping their chins on their crossed feet which dangled over their heads, they started walking about on their hands. I couldn't take my eyes off my Delfina, now sitting perfectly normally on a chair. Only that all at once she spread her arms and without altering the position of her legs swivelled her upper body right round and clasped the back of the chair.

They were two freaks of nature capable of the most impossible movements, with detachable joints and retractable limbs. Delfina seemed more made of rubber than ever. Supple as a snake, she twisted herself into a writhing knot on the floor, bent like a worm on the hook. Pointing her feet to form a tail, and bringing the tip to her mouth, she spun back and forth like a hubcap. She whirled so fast I thought she would crash into the wall.

Instead she abruptly checked herself and got to her feet. I was watching from behind, with no more than five paces between us. Bending over from the waist she grasped her knees. All at once her face appeared between her legs, but not upside down, right way up, suspended in the air, for all the world like the disembodied head of a dwarf girl. I wasn't sure she was looking at me, she held the position so long she was possibly just taking a break. Yet I still couldn't avoid the feeling I was being stared at. Her twin crept towards her with the menacing movements of a crocodile, quick then slow, in spurts, arms and legs projecting from his trunk.

I couldn't think straight, I felt trapped in a labyrinth with no notion what to do, nothing to help me find my bearings. I couldn't even summon the strength to get to my feet and leave, flee. I shut my eyes and when I opened them again I saw Delfina shrinking to the size of a small bundle, a black ball. Her brother picked the ball up in his two hands and slipped it into a wooden crate no bigger than a cardboard wine carrier. He popped the lid back on, picked it up and went over to his bed where he set it down in place of a bedside table, putting a small lamp and a digital alarm clock on top. Then he turned and looked full at me.

My first impulse was to hurl myself at him, so insulted did I feel by the whole performance. It struck me as the most crass and perverse message, the total opposite of our carefree way of meeting on the street, and our mild and well-mannered, almost insubstantial talk. The total opposite of their monstrous gymnastics. I was deeply hurt, and as I left I slammed the door behind me.

I've never seen them again, I made a point of taking the metro in Via Ottaviano just to avoid them. All the same, I find present memories are not as sour as the unpleasant impression they made on me at the time. Once in a while I think of them quite fondly, even with a touch of nostalgia. Still, Delfina's contorted world would never have suited mine.

The Beautiful Hand

Giorgio Vigolo

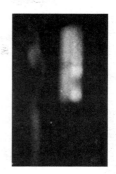

For all who chance to be born in memorable cities, ancient and vast as worlds, and have lived there long, nothing is more fascinating and absorbing than opening up memories of our earliest years of life half lost in dreams. We no longer quite know whether we are recalling events we actually lived through or which go back further, pre-dating ourselves, gleaned from who knows what chronicle or the lips of the very last witnesses, read in the stones or house façades, or conjured by the last light in some solitary corner of the city where around dusk it always seems something of the past is repeating itself, as though the aura and awe of long-gone events can rework them still.

Then inevitably one calls to mind other discoveries made over time in other parts of the city which not all at once but only little by little has yielded up something more of itself in often unexpected encounters, as when in my own city I first happened upon previously unknown piazzas.

Hunting down early recollections can become a passion to renew these old surprises buried in memory, digging deep within oneself for the *first apparitions* of certain places in the city. How was it for me, for instance, living at the opposite and furthest end of the city on the other bank of the Tiber, when for the first time Piazza del Laterano appeared to me, silent and immense, with its great obelisk and palaces, the age-old basilica with its loggia and twin steepled bell-towers? Only the intensest effort of concentration might perhaps retrieve a little of the life and colour still lingering in me from that faded vision, so remote now that it merges with the many scenes and episodes I have imagined since, and visualized as actually present, which occurred right there in the Lateran during the High Middle Ages. Fantasy and memory, dream and history are inextricably entangled, yet still the feeling persists of somehow actually journeying back through time, beyond one's own existence, back to the impersonal, to *all the light remembers* of the places on which it has shone for so many centuries.

I spoke of 'opening up'. Obscurely, when unwittingly writing that phrase, I was thinking of a window from which I experienced a vision of blinding radiance, like the sea when you come out of a tunnel. I must have been still very little. I had been taken to Via dell'Anima to visit some people of note in their gloomy apartment situated inside an enormous palace. Via dell'Anima well deserves its name; it is an other-worldly street, dark and deep, squeezed between tall buildings, between a church and a crenellated medieval tower. On grey days the sky overhead courses like livid liquid silver between the bleak, perpendicular banks of the houses. On wet days the rain drenching the walls forms stains in which vanished frescos appear to seep through the plaster—flashing eyes and the bewitched faces of women from other times seem to stare out at you.

Entering the forbidding portal, climbing the staircase and then passing through the darkened rooms of the vast building, I was going through my tunnel, though with no thought or presentiment of all the light on the other side, of what a contrast lay in store for me as though deliberately devised by some friendly genius leading me to discover Rome by subtle pathways and with the keenest sense of adventure.

The surprise awaiting me when I looked out from the side opposite the Via dell'Anima was nothing less than the great ellipse of Piazza Navona, with its three fountains. Of all this I still retain a clear picture, a crystalline original in the atlas of memory, and so can be sure beyond all doubt that was the first time the famous panorama appeared to me.

But my memory does not stop there; it is intertwined with the mood and history of the palace itself which gradually came to cast a spell over me too, for I was to return many times after that first visit, in fact I used to beg to go back there particularly on evenings round Christmas and Twelfth Night when the piazza had an almost saturnalian atmosphere of revelry, enlivened even more at night by all the lights and colourful reflections from the stalls full of Christmas crib figures, corks and lichens, stars and silver comets, and beyond them the shooting booths and the sweet and candyfloss stands. All this you could look down on as from a box in a theatre.

The great attraction the windows onto the piazza held for me, however, was offset by the dark and at bottom fearful impression made on me by the palace interior with its immense rooms with high ceilings lost in shadow, the statues and busts in the hallway, and most of all by a great drawing room hung with tapestries where it truly seemed previous inhabitants were invisibly confined, still not quite able to detach themselves from the scenes of their lives.

But these vague feelings came to converge upon and assume almost living form in the cast of an exceptionally beautiful female hand, breathtaking in its grace and poise, glowing white as snow inside a glass urn in the drawing room. It was displayed on deep crimson velvet and although discontinued above the wrist expressed a beauty and serenity I would call almost physiognomic, as though smiling in complete repose, and with the power to evoke, provoke, the entire breathing presence of the woman to whom it must have belonged. On the cusp between childhood and earliest adolescence, I would stand spellbound before that glass, and I am certain it was then that I received the first indelible revelation of female beauty, in that naked hand lying open on velvet.

The family retained little more than a vague legend about the hand. They spoke of a lady of noble birth who had lived long ago in those very rooms, and who on account of her beautiful hands had suffered some grim fate about which no one remembered anything precise. The unsettling effect of the legend was enhanced by their fanciful and vaguely magical and superstitious conviction that, if I can so put it, *the ghost of the hand haunted* the rooms of the ancient palace. Indeed on one of those winter nights round Christmas when Piazza Navona beneath me surged with crowds, they managed to shock me too when someone suddenly pointed out the hand to me, gracious and quite alone, shimmering on the sill of a window, as though breathing inside a faint iridescent pearly glow, its own tiny supernatural nocturnal rainbow. Next instant the hand had moved, no longer to be seen on the sill but in the shadowy depths of a mirror on a table nearby.

'You're all so stupid!' shouted behind us the oldest of my little friends who had never had any patience with the tales of apparitions. 'Can't you see it's the moon? First it lit up the marble of the windowsill and now it's reflecting from the floor into the mirror!'

Perhaps it was so. The December moon was rising full and clear in the chill winter sky, and already half Piazza Navona was bathed in its light between the black shadows of the buildings and the white of the statues, and the spurting fountains in which the lunar rays refracted the same nocturnal rainbow.

But, as always happens, one person's incredulity excited and stimulated the others' fantasies. One evening, in fact, I was led on tiptoe into the dark drawing room and, not without a shiver, was convinced I could see the hand's pearly glow inside the glass urn; a faint phosphorescence seemed to etch its shape, intensifying for an instant like the lunar rainbow on the windowsill. Then the halo round the hand faded, the drawing room was plunged in darkness again, closed upon itself, and I stole away pervaded by a delicious dread in which terror of death and the afterlife mingled with the fascination of a being of extraordinary beauty. And since it is precisely in such states of mind, favoured by the particular associations of ancient and memorable places which breed legends like forests of ivy on ruins, little by little in the palace on Piazza Navona similarly began to grow up a wondrous belief in the ghostly apparitions of the hand, and an astronomical occurrence became attached to the legend, a place in the calendar, linking it mysteriously with the moon. In nights when the moon was full, not only would the beautiful hand appear on windowsills and in the depths of mirrors, but the cast itself would glow in the dark of the drawing room within its elusive opalescent rainbow.

A great many years have gone by since then, and still every time I passed that way I could not resist glancing up at the window on whose sill I had once seen the beautiful hand appear. I would stand there a minute or two and relive that distant episode from childhood with the keener curiosity which had superseded my old apprehension without dispelling it altogether. Since the old houses of Rome are impregnated with a mysterious impersonal memory, and superstitious notions and fables and legends are like the dreams of their walls, it is hard not to believe that they must have remote roots in real events. In any case, I would reflect that even if mirrors and the moon all too easily favour ghostly or fantastic apparitions, the repetition of the strange mirage still required explanation, and in particular why it was so attached to those windows, and to that house, and not somewhere else.

It is not difficult, therefore, to appreciate my astonishment the day it became clear from certain documents and chronicles dating from the early seventeenth century that the house I used to visit as a boy (to be precise, that still standing on the west side of the piazza between Via dei Lorenesi and Via Sant'Agnese) had been none other than the palace of Cardinal De Cupis, known as the Cardinal of Trani, who in the sixteenth century had had it erected over an area where a number of more modest dwellings had been demolished. In the early years of the next century, one of his great-nephews had married and brought to live in the palace on Piazza Navona one of the most beautiful women in Rome: Costanza, of the noble Conti family, the sister of Lotario, Duke of Poli. This lady (and here my heart truly missed a beat and my childhood recollections as it were sparked a sudden lightning flash of memory to illuminate the past) was famed for possessing hands of extraordinary beauty.

Contemporary chroniclers all concur in praising the beauty of her hands, claiming they were fashioned by nature with such inspiration and delicacy as to dim even her face and figure which were themselves of remarkable beauty. They also add that Costanza was perhaps just a little too pleased with them; a pardonable vanity when one remembers that a perfect hand is a gift even rarer than a most beautiful face. Still, it seems the judgement of her contemporaries was not so clement, for around this very point they weave the dark thread of her destiny whereby, as in so many other instances, beauty becomes a fateful gift tempting death.

What is beyond dispute is that in the year 1618, possibly yielding to some admirer's pleas, Costanza agreed to have a cast made of her hands, and it may be supposed not without reluctance and some sense of foreboding. The best moulder in Rome at the time was *Bastiano alli Serpenti*, that is 'Bastiano at the sign of the Serpents', of whom a chronicler of the time has preserved the name along with the singular story of what happened to Costanza after the casts of her hands were taken.

To situate these events more precisely, however, we must change district of Rome and leave Parione for the steep medieval district of Monti, attempting to picture it at the time when Bastiano the moulder had his shop here 'opposite the church of Madonna Santissima dei Monti, in the house of the serpents'. It is a corner of the old city still traceable on Antonio Tempesta's 'Plan of Rome', along the street which still today bears the name of Via dei Serpenti. The Monti district, as the name infers, runs up and down in steep rises and sudden drops which in those days gave it an even more thrilling appearance rich in changing perspectives, and still today, along with the street names, arouses memories of the medieval barons, their ambushes and their battles: the Annibaldi fortified in the Colosseum, the Conti and the Crescenzi with their tall towers, the Ciacaleoni and the Capocci. Presiding over and dominating all this hilly area, secluded high above it and flanked by a fine basilica with a five-arched portico, lies Piazza San Pietro in Vincoli, directly beneath which once rose the residence of the Borgias. The antique statue of Laocoön was discovered here in a nearby vineyard from where we are told it was borne in triumph, festooned in roses, all through the streets of the city.

The house where the moulder Bastiano had his work-shop owed its name to a Laocoön with the snakes wrapped round him painted on the façade. It is therefore more than likely that Bastiano, supreme in his profession, had made a cast of the famous group, and then used the Laocoön fresco as his shop sign. We also know 'the house with the painted snakes' was owned by a certain Flaminio Cerasola and that there was an inn in the same building, and 'innkeeper Francesco lived here'. These names from long ago are curiously evocative and together with the precise details of the location combine to conjure up a clear picture of this spot in the city, so that one can seem almost to see again the frontage of the Cerasola building as it was then, with its painted Laocoön struggling inside the serpents' coils, and on one side the inn and on the other Bastiano's shop.

So we are in the year 1618. Now let us try to enter the picture ourselves and mount the three steps and take a look inside the shop. Amid the many casts of statues and the great white Laocoön standing in a corner, right there on the counter, posed as I used to see the one inside the glass urn, lie the hands of Costanza dei Conti. The casts are so beautiful that word has spread fast and many people have come to see them, laymen and clergy and nobility have all been calling by to gaze on them in wonder.

That same summer evening, one of the canons regular of San Pietro in Vincoli leaves his quarters in the monastery next to the basilica and ducking into the vaulted archway which supports the Borgia houses goes down the long steep stairway there, then turns right along Via Urbana towards Via dei Serpenti. Who knows whether his goal was indeed Bastiano's shop, or whether as he went past he was struck by the unusual throng of people in there and out of curiosity stepped inside. In any case, in the shop at that same moment was another characteristic figure of those early years of the seventeenth century, the memoirist Antonio Valera, one of those referred to earlier, and who was therefore witness to the event and noted it down in his *Cose memorabili.* He saw the canon come in and halt in front of the counter where the casts of the beautiful hands were lying, then pick one up to examine it more closely. As to all appearances he was engaged in intensely scrutinizing the lines in the palm of this left hand, he suddenly frowned and something clouded his features, and as though thinking out loud to himself he uttered the following words: 'This beautiful hand, if it belongs to someone living, is in danger of being cut off.' 'Knowing whose it was,' adds Antonio at this point in his account, 'I laughed at the remark.'

I must confess I would not have shared his laughter, for in the canon's words I am certain I detect the declaration of a ferocious anathema, albeit couched in the sibylline terms of a chiromancer's prognosis; unless we are to believe that in the lines of that hand he actually could read cryptic events and the germ of a tragic fate. Equally, I must confess that many times returning to that spot I have endeavoured to compel it to grant me some fuller and more illuminating memory of the facts. And each time I have seemed to see Costanza secretly make her way up to the basilica of San Pietro in Vincoli to seek out the canon whose sinister prediction had been passed from mouth to mouth and eventually reached her ears; and that the canon, rather than mitigate his response and allay her fears, had magnified her anguish by pitilessly condemning the sinfulness of permitting a cast of her hands to be made, which to his eyes was pagan worship of her own beauty exposed for others to adore. Far better were it to have cut off that too beautiful hand than let it corrupt and poison her soul.

From that moment on Costanza could find no peace of mind: she felt under a curse from which she would never free herself, her own beauty had become a nightmare to her.

And so it was that some time later, still racked by anguish, she sought purification and penance in a task which both distracted her and kept her occupied: she set herself to embroider a pattern of lilies on a purple chasuble for the neighbouring church of Sant'Agnese in Agone. Late one afternoon she was alone at the window intent on her embroidery, and looking out over the lovely square she felt her spirits rise, and for a moment forgot her woe: from the houses opposite, on the eastern side of the piazza, light reflected from the setting sun came flooding in. She saw her hands lit up against the blood-red dazzle of purple and they seemed to her more beautiful than ever, so beautiful she suddenly took fright, and at that same moment she distinctly seemed to hear that terrible voice repeating: 'Far better were it to have cut off that hand...'

With the sudden shock which ran right through her it was as though a destructive and vengeful will had forced entry, and she drove the needle deep in, impaling her living flesh. At first it seemed almost nothing, but the wound became infected, the beautiful hand became swollen and deformed. It turned black. To save her life there was no alternative but amputation, but this failed to ward off the greater evil, for Costanza died from it shortly after.

Thus ends Antonio Valena's chronicle, with which Amidenio's account in Latin concurs in every point, without adding anything more.

Can it be there were further reasons to be found in Costanza's life of which we have no knowledge, and which the chroniclers leave unsaid? Was she asked for the cast of her hands by someone to whom she then secretly gave them as a symbol of the commitment of the whole of herself? Did this augment her sense of her own sinfulness and obscurely provoke the fatal self-mutilation? Unfortunately we cannot know and never shall, unless some unforeseeable light is shed on it some day from who knows where, from some exchange of letters concealed in a sacristy or monastery, or some noble household. All we know is that the memory and legend of that singular beauty linked to a mysterious fatality has passed down through the centuries as far as ourselves in the episodes I have given. Costanza de Cupis is one of Rome's legendary women; like Beatrice Cenci's head*,

---

* Beatrice was tortured and executed by order of Pope Clement VII in 1599 with other family members for complicity in the murder of her monstrous father.

her hand was severed by a perverse judgement, though in a more covert manner in her case. And in my childhood I lived in the wake of her last fantastic manifestation, surrounded by the aura of her presence I looked out from the window of her fatal embroidery.

But perhaps one day the walls of the palace on Piazza Navona will speak, or some night amid the moon's reflections in the waterdrops and the iridescent play of the fountains Costanza will appear to a poet and reveal the full secret of her suffering.

The Girl with the Braid

Dacia Maraini

A girl of fifteen is walking up Viale Bruno Buozzi. Her steps are hurried yet hesitant. She walks hunched into herself, with some perplexing thought lurking behind the arcs of her eyebrows. You can easily picture her: on the small side, something slightly wonky about her spindly legs, with wide shoulders, thin neck, a tiny head. The girl you picture has the slenderest waist, at her last school they called her 'ant' because it's small enough to squeeze between two hands. She has brown hair and it hangs in a braid down the middle of her back.

The girl arrived in the city a very few months ago from a village in the midst of the mountains. And to her the streets of Rome are so long she fears she could easily lose her way, the cafés so brightly lit she still sometimes mistakes them for jewellers', the houses so high just looking at them makes her dizzy.

The girl with the braid spent three years shut in a convent school up there in the mountains. Encased in a shapeless itchy blue woollen uniform, she had filed two by two with the other girls through the village streets. She had looked longingly at the sun rising between rocky crags. She had rubbed Nivea cream into her chilblains, wondering why she was ever born. She had so loved a dog called Leone and it had died deaf and blind of old age.

That day in May the girl with the braid was walking up Viale Bruno Buozzi searching for a number, number one hundred and thirty-one. It kept coming to her lips: one, three, one; and then in other combinations: thirteen plus one, one hundred plus thirty plus one... one hundred and thirty-one. At that number she would find the doctor who would help her to... She couldn't say the word, her tongue stuck to the roof of her mouth. How could such an immature body contain an even less mature body, so tiny it didn't yet even have any recognizable shape? A creature which all the same she felt somehow distinct from herself, as tenuous as a faraway captive voice snickering crazily in some corner of her stomach. How come it was laughing? Didn't it know that very soon it would have to be dislodged from its warm hidey-hole and go blowing away through the cold clear streets of the sky swept by quick-silver winds?

Probably it was chuckling about her, the fifteen-year-old with the braid bobbing against her back walking up Viale Bruno Buozzi looking for a number made up of a one, a three, and another one.

As her gym shoes pressed into the sun-softened asphalt the girl asked herself who might have fathered the little laughing creature. Since coming to Rome she had led a disorganized life full of surprises and revelations.

She had gone out with a certain Vaccarella, a glum young man with gold-rimmed spectacles and dark blue suits, who took her to expensive restaurants and ate without saying a word while squeezing her hand under the tablecloth, then took her to a hotel on Piazza Barberini to make love like two married people, with painstaking fastidiousness. Afterwards, he would dress just as neat and tidy as before, tie, waistcoat, blue jacket, and escort her to the taxi without saying a word.

Vaccarella might well be the father of the baby which would surely turn out just as sad and polite as him, as precise as him, and as without hopes as him. Vaccarella had a wife, he had confessed to it in a low voice one evening while smoking a cigarette after love in the room in the hotel on Piazza Barberini. He loved this wife 'as much as himself' was how he put it, and she had thought he couldn't love himself very much.

Even in love he was cheerless and meticulous. He removed his clothes one by one. He folded his trousers neatly over the chair making sure the creases lined up. Every time he hung his trousers over the back of the chair the coins slipped out of the pockets and went rolling all over the floor with a merry tinkle. And every time he reddened as at some terrible misdeed. Then he would bend over in his shirt and underpants and patiently gather up all the coins, setting them one by one on the bed.

The girl had wondered if she was in love with young Vaccarella but had had to answer in the negative. And yet she had been swept off her feet by him, by that ink-blue suit smelling faintly of sandalwood aftershave. She had been seduced by his silence and his pallor. Is it possible to fall in love with the pallor of a man's face?—she'd thought the first time she saw him waiting for her outside school pacing nervously up and down with a lighted cigarette between his fingers.

She had been struck at once by his hairy wrists and that dark pained look in his eyes as of someone who was once beaten within an inch of his life and however hard he tries can never get it out of his mind. It had struck her how drained he was of colour, as though his face had been gone over again and again with a rubber until every line was erased.

But what if instead it was Professor Gaetani's baby? It had only happened once, and the girl wondered if that was enough. The workings of conception were not too clear to her. Her mother, who thought of herself as a modern woman, had said, 'Always be careful, take the proper precautions.' But what these precautions were she had not explained, either out of modesty or because she imagined young girls like her knew everything already.

It was true they knew everything, but in a hazy abstract fashion. There was always the solid fact that the Madonna had had a baby without making love. And among the girls in the village in the mountains this generated a vague unease. Besides, there was much talk of a certain Pina who although she had done no more than pet with her boy without actually copulating had still ended up pregnant. Something must happen when kissing, perhaps through the saliva, they decided. Or perhaps through his flying seed. Hadn't they been told a man's seed can jump like salmon when they make their way up rivers right to the source to find a safe place to deposit their precious burden? The danger of an unwanted pregnancy hung over the girls' heads like divine grace which any time can catch you unawares.

Professor Gaetani had a way of entering the classroom invariably late and all unshaven with his shirt only half tucked in, his jumper inside out, and his hair plastered down flat on one side in a way which amused the girls. Rushing in like a tramp off the street made him look almost handsome. His eyes went big and shiny, his tensed lips flashed a fixed smile of acute embarrassment. He looked like he'd just landed from the moon and was gazing around him in disbelief at the novelty of this world.

One morning it had chanced just the two of them were left in the classroom. He had stared at her like he'd never seen her before, with a gleam of appreciation in his weary pupils. She had thought she would never again love any man with the veneration and the tenderness she felt for him that moment.

The teacher, with the temerity of the timid, had seized her hand. And immediately she had longed to be gobbled up by him, as though beneath that blundering scatter-brained exterior she had sensed the remorseless and in-nocent cravings of a cannibal.

She had wondered if he too loved her. And for a moment it had seemed so. As she saw him make quietly for the door tugging her by the hand it had seemed he really did love her. They had leaned up against the door to make sure no one burst in on them. And there, wrapped in each other's arms, they had kissed one another tenderly a long time.

Two days later Professor Gaetani had signalled to her as the pupils were preparing to leave and she had understood she had to follow him to his car parked two streets away.

As soon as the door was shut he had driven off at speed with a greedy little wolfish smile playing on his lips. The car, swift and supple as a tadpole, had squirmed its way into the great river of traffic in Viale Trastevere, and then on through Piazza Sonnino, Vicolo San Gallicano, Piazza Santa Apollonia to Vicolo della Pelliccia.

Her teacher talked and talked but seemingly without listening to what he was saying. Strained, airy talk. It was as if he strove to mesmerize her with the fascination of his voice, as a snake charmer forces his reptile to dance by playing his flute.

Professor Gaetano had talked incessantly all through his lovemaking. Lapsing silent only when he abruptly opened his eyes wide and collapsed against her shoulder with a hoarse groan.

He started talking again while she took a shower and pulled her clothes back on. What he had talked about with such manic distraction was hard to recall. He talked about her, about her extreme youth which was both a danger and an attraction, he had quoted poets called Archilochus and Mimnermus and then told about a cat called Ciccio who had got lost somewhere among the rooftops of Via Pelliccia.

Still talking, he had given her a lift to the bus stop. 'It's best they don't see us together outside your house,' he'd said. And while kissing her he had looked right into her eyes as though to say: 'I'll never let you go.'

Next day Professor Gaetani didn't come to school, nor the day after that. The girl with the dark brown braid thought it was 'all because of her' he hadn't come and she felt divinely 'guilty'. The supply teacher said he was ill. She pictured him in bed, in the darkness of that messy house, eating his heart out for her.

Instead Professor Gaetani hadn't come to school because he'd gone off on a trip with his young wife. She only got to hear of it some time later. He'd been playing truant, that was all.

Next week he had showed up in class again with his usual dishevelled absent-minded air, eyes fixed on the floor, smile intense. He had not even given her so much as a glance and as soon as the bell went he dashed out without a parting word to anyone.

Days, weeks, went by without him addressing a single word to her. In the end she'd decided to go and wait for him outside his house just to talk things over a bit.

After waiting two hours she'd seen him come out of his front door hugging his beautiful young wife. He had glanced in her direction for a moment but had immediately turned away pretending not to see her.

So could the baby really be Professor Gaetani's? Could she ever even have told him? She seemed to see it, a teenager already, shirt dangling out of its trousers, shoes shapeless, the same sharp nose, the same long delicate fingers. And what if it was a baby girl instead? But the girl just couldn't imagine a daughter looking like Professor Gaetani. Would she have worn her blouse outside her skirt? Would she too have a pointy nose and long delicate fingers? Would she too twist her lips into a little wolfish grin?

Imagine a girl with a long heavy braid bobbing against the middle of her back walking a bit hunched in on herself up the long slope of Viale Bruno Buozzi. Imagine her intent on something, her face almost disfigured by a distressing thought: why sever herself from that baby she can already hear chortling under the soft curves of her stomach?

Now the girl with the antlike waist sits down on a low wall bordering the pavement, just at the spot where two dusty locust trees grow a bit wonkily. Her gaze fixes on some sun-scorched blades of grass. In the middle of the grass, like a drop of blood, is a radiant poppy, so beautiful. Since when have poppies started growing in cities?—she wonders to herself. In actual fact it's the tiniest poppy, a bit stunted as if only born by chance, against all odds, from a single seed cast into the air and then blown all over the place by a spiteful and uncaring wind. It had come up poor and stunted, but it had come up. Who would ever dream of pulling it out?

A quick glance at her watch alarms her: the appointment is in just two minutes. But what was the house number? There was a one and a three, this she clearly remembers, but then what? She has forgotten. And she has forgotten the doctor's name as well.

Can it be that her craving for company is playing tricks with her memory? Her craving to go on listening to that soft chortling, even if malign, even if mocking, but that and no other, and with those queer undercurrents of rage?

You're fifteen, she says to herself, you're almost through your last year at school, and you're expecting a baby and don't know whose it is—who can you tell about it? Perhaps her mother would say to keep it. Just to bring it up herself. But her father would stare at her out of an uncomprehending swollen face, with hurt, sick eyes. It's queer how much he looks like Professor Gaetani, she'd never noticed that before, but it really is so. They even have the same long delicate hands.

The number comes back to her with sudden clarity. Her feet all by themselves start walking again. The braid once more starts bobbing softly against her back in time with those childish strides. But where is she going? That road won't take her to the doctor's house. Where is she going?

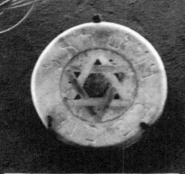

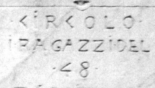

CIRCOLO
I RAGAZZI DEL
·48·
·Z I RAIMONDO·

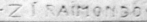
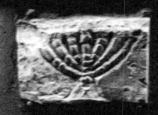

16 October 1943

Giacomo Debenedetti

A mysterious figure, about whom it would be interesting to have more information, shows up at the Community offices on 11 October at the head of an SS detachment. At first sight he would seem to be a German officer like any other, though with an extra dose of arrogance due to his membership of a privileged and woefully renowned 'special force'. All uniform from top to toe: that tight-fitting uniform of such a fastidious, abstract, and inflexible elegance that it seals up the person inside, their physical and above all moral self, with the hermetic efficiency of a zip fastener. He is the word *verboten* made uniform: forbidden to trespass upon the individual and the specific past alive in him which is his unique story and his more authentic 'special force' as a creature of this world;

forbidden to glimpse anything other than this severe, robotic, unbending *presence.*

While his men start pulling apart the libraries in the Rabbinical College and the Community, with the meticulous care of a fine embroiderer the officer fingers and fondles and smoothes out papyri and incunabula, leafs through manuscripts and rare editions, eases open parchment codices and palimpsests. The caution with which he handles them, the pressure of his touch, is instantly adjusted to the merits of the volume. For the most part the works are written in remote alphabets. Yet on opening a page the officer's gaze will at once focus and light up, as happens only with certain exceptionally well-equipped readers who can instinctively hit on the passage they hope for, the revealing extract. In those refined hands, as though exposed to extreme yet bloodless torture of the subtlest sadism, the books talk. Later it was learned that the SS officer was an eminent scholar of Semitic palaeography and philology.

The library of the Rabbinical College in Rome, and that of the Community even more, contained superlative collections and outstanding single volumes, some of them unique. A thoroughgoing study and catalogue had not yet been undertaken, but in all likelihood would have revealed further treasures. To our knowledge, both libraries housed extensive documents and manuscript and printed chronicles concerning the Diaspora in the Mediterranean basin, as well as all the most authentic sources for the entire history right from earliest times of the Jews in Rome, the closest and most direct descendants of ancient Judaism. Unknown accounts from as yet unexplored angles of the Rome of the Caesars and of the later emperors and popes lay hidden within those writings. And generations which truly seem to have passed through this world like the race of leaves waited in the depths of those pages for someone to let them speak.

A crisp tug of the zip, and the uniform has locked away the Semitist who is once more an officer in the SS. He orders: anyone touching, concealing, or removing so much as one of these books will be summarily shot in accordance with the German rule of war. He leaves. The sound of his heels echoes on the stairs. Within a very short while, utilizing the tramlines of the Circolare Nera, three goods wagons draw up. The SS load the two libraries inside. The wagons depart. Books, manuscripts, codices, and parchments are on their way to Munich.

Who knows if they were the same wagons whose task it would shortly be to take another, and in a far different sense, vital consignment to Germany. There was time to make it there and back: five days. And here once again one cannot help but ask, as though the question could even now still alert those it most concerns: if such

outrages* continued to occur why did no one think of
fleeing? True, the theft of the books was no outrage to the
people of the Ghetto, who knew nothing about books. On
the other hand it was these same inhabitants of 'Piazza
Giudia' who should have most sensed the threat, since
they were destined to furnish the greatest haul of victims.
Yet would they even have heeded the warning? They had
grown indolent, profoundly attached to their locality. The
Wandering Jew is worn out by now, he has walked far
enough, he is exhausted. The strain of so many exiles and
flights and deportations, of the many, many roads
tramped by their ancestors over centuries and centuries,
has ended up by blighting the muscles of their children;
their legs refuse to drag their flat feet one step further.
Besides, and let no one doubt it, a fifth column was
working hard to 'spread trust'. For instance, on 9 October
a considerable number of Jews had been arrested. Many
were frightened, it could have signalled the onset of a

* Just three weeks earlier the people of the Ghetto ('Piazza Giudia') had been
given two days to hand over fifty kilos of gold to the German high command
or face the instant deportation to Germany of two hundred from their
community, for being 'guilty twice over, as Italians for betraying Germany,
and as Jews for belonging to the race of Germany's eternal enemies' (Debenedetti). Mussolini had been deposed by his own Fascist Grand Council on
25 July, and on 8 September, after secret negotiations with the Allies and
despite the massive presence of German troops in Italy, the new government
under Marshal Badoglio announced the nation had capitulated and now
sided with its former enemies. Fascist diehards sided with the Germans,
particularly after Mussolini's installation as puppet head of government in
German-occupied Italy, some zealously aiding in the persecution of the Jews.

general persecution. In response, the reassuring information (and persons in positions of authority in the Community, though indisputably with the best of intentions, aided its propagation) was promptly put about that these arrests were exceptional and strictly circumscribed, being all of persons already identified as active anti-fascists. The activity had been targeted, not the race. The Germans continued to appear reasonable, almost human. Given their overwhelming power, their authority so absolute, *they could have done far worse.* Instead . . . No, there was no special cause to mistrust them, no need to overdramatize.

So the Jews were sleeping soundly in their beds when around midnight on Friday 15 October the roads outside erupted with gunfire and detonations. Ever since 25 July when Badoglio had imposed the curfew, and after 8 September even more, shots had been heard in the streets almost every night, generally assumed to involve people circulating without a permit out of hours. But the usual gunshots had been far apart, like the hourly chimes, and seldom this close, and never so persistent. These instead intensify, accelerate, overlap, escalating into a veritable shoot out. And would they were just gunshots, for something more sinister is mixed in with them: sharp bangs which then spread out like waves, as though opening a doleful ever-widening crater in the darkness. *Barùch dajàn emèd*,* it's like being in the middle of a battle. Some sit up in bed.

The bravest venture to the windows. Bullets and fragments of masonry are whistling and whining barely inches off the shutters, or thudding into the ancient plaster on the outer walls. Through the slats in the shutters and the thickening drizzle, among the flicker of gunfire and flash of explosives down in the street, squads of soldiers can be glimpsed shooting in the air and tossing hand grenades at the pavements. By their helmets they would seem to be Germans; but there was only time for a cursory look, it would be unwise to stay by the window. And now the *jorbatìm* are commencing to call out and yell too: their voices and their cries are shrill, irate, sarcastic, and incomprehensible. What do they want? Who do they have it in for? Where are they going?

In all the houses everyone is up by now. Neighbouring families meet up for reassurance, and instead only manage to frighten each other more. Their children scream. But what can you say to calm children when you yourselves don't know what to say to each other? Stop crying, they're going off towards Monte Savello now, they're going to Piazza Cairoli, it will soon all be over, you'll see. But it is anything but over. They had seemed to be moving away,

---

* Hebrew: 'Blessed be the Judge of Truth.' In the next paragraph, *Jorbatìm*: 'soldiers'.

but now they're back, and all this time the shooting has never stopped. If only they'd do something, break in a door, smash a shutter, a shop, at least then we'd know what it's all about. But no, they fire off their guns, they shrill, and that's all. It's like toothache, you don't know how long it will last or how much worse it can get. This incomprehension is the worst of nightmares. A woman who gave birth only hours ago can stand the torment no longer, she scrambles out of bed, grabs the baby, dashes into the front room next door, but then passes out. The women rush to her aid: cognac, a hot water bottle, this at least is everyday life, the sort of affliction you know how to cope with. But the people out there have not stopped shooting and shrieking for two hours, three hours, more than three.

Every year at the Passover meal—'let all who hunger come and eat'—half of an unleavened bread is always set aside. A belief handed down since time immemorial, perhaps from when the Jews were still farming people, holds that a morsel of this unleavened bread thrown from a window will propitiate the hurricanes, tempests, and hailstorms which destroy the bread, strip the vines and olive trees, and bring famine and very possibly death. Who knows whether anyone that night considered taking from its drawer the unleavened bread saved up from the previous Passover—when, for the last time, they had commemorated the flight from Egypt and liberation from the Pharaohs—to hurl it against that mayhem. The corn was reaped, the grapes gathered, but another harvest had still to be brought safely in, the children of Israel whom the patriarchs had been assured would be as numberless as the sand upon the shore. Yet had that innocent morsel dropped from a window, the Germans would have trained their carbines and sub-machine guns on the window, and flung their hand grenades at it.

Only they knew the reason for that inferno. But perhaps the true reason was simply that there was none at all: a gratuitous inferno, to appear more mysterious, and so more intimidating. There and then, people presumed it was an act of spite, a joke against the Jews. Later, with the logic and wisdom of hindsight, it was decided the Germans meant to terrify the people of the Ghetto, and—in case something had leaked out about plans for the morrow—force them to stay battened inside their homes, and thus take them all.

At around four in the morning the shooting subsided. It was cold, the damp of the rainy night penetrated the walls. What with that brutal awakening, everyone had remained in nightclothes and slippers, with at most a thin shawl or an overcoat over their shoulders. The beds they had forsaken still perhaps retained a little warmth. Exhausted, with that hollow dried-out feeling which extreme stress leaves in the eye sockets, bones aching, teeth chattering, all made their way back to their own homes and beds. In two hours it would be daylight, then finally they'd get some answers. On the other hand, when all is said and done, *nothing had actually happened.*

It seems the first to raise the alarm was a woman called Letizia, known to the neighbourhood as Letizia Bug-Eyes: an overweight elderly woman with the mind of a child, with bloated features and figure and popping eyes. Big turned-up lips print an expressionless smile on her face and between them issues a faraway tetchy voice bearing no relation to the words it utters. At around five o'clock she was heard to shout:

'Oh God, the *mammoni*!'

'Mammoni' in Roman-Jewish slang means the cops, the police, officers of the law. In fact they are the Germans, who with their heavy rhythmic tread (we know people for whom this beat has become the symbol, the chilling auditory equivalent of the German terror) have begun blocking off streets and houses in the Ghetto. The owner of a small café in the Portico di Ottavia—an 'Aryan' who from the vantage point of his premises was able to witness every stage of the operation as it unfolded—arrived shortly before from Testaccio, where he lives. Making his way through Monte Savello and along the Portico he had noticed nothing abnormal. (Would it have been possible to slip away after the shooting ceased, or was the whole quarter already surrounded?) He says he began to hear that rhythmic pounding of boots at around five-thirty (it has proved impossible to get witnesses to agree on the timescale, that catastrophic time must have been terribly elastic, susceptible only to psychological calculation). At this point he hadn't yet opened the premises, he was starting up the espresso machine: he unfastened a shutter, and saw.

He saw ranged down both pavements two long lines of Germans: a good hundred, at a guess. In the middle of the road stood officers posting armed sentries to all corners of the street. A few passers-by had stopped to watch. The Germans had no interest in them. Only later did they start seizing anyone carrying bundles or suitcases, telltale signs of attempted flight.

In her flat in Via Sant'Ambrogio, at around five (psychological time, again) Signora Laurina S. is hailed from the street. It's a niece of hers shouting:

'Auntie, Auntie, come down! The Germans are taking everyone away!'

Moments before, coming out of her house in Via della Reginella, this girl had seen an entire family with six children, the eldest just ten, being led away. Signora S. leans out of the window. On either side of the front door she sees two Germans armed with carbines (or sub-machine guns, she can't specify). It may well be wondered how her niece could possibly have called up from the road like that, and so explicitly, right in front of two Germans (the street is claustrophobically narrow, just an alleyway). We repeat, in the main the Germans did not seize people in the street: outside of their own homes, only those unfortunates more or less asking to be picked up were taken. Nor should it be supposed the tragedy took place in an atmosphere of hushed and dumbfounded solemnity: people carried on talking amongst themselves, calling out information and advice, just as in normal everyday life. Fate conducted its portentous work without standing on ceremony, without insisting on good behaviour. Drama entered into and mingled with life with frightening naturalness, scarcely leaving room even for stupefaction at the time.

At first Signora S. supposed, like everyone, that the Germans had come to remove the men for 'labour service'. This notion, probably spread deliberately, was the ruin of many families who did not think to save older men and women and children. At all events, trusting in the presumed immunity of women, Signora S. takes heart, pulls on some clothes, grabs ration books and shopping bag, and heads downstairs to discover what's going on. A day or two earlier she'd had a fall, she's trailing a leg in plaster.

Down on the street, she approaches the Germans on sentry duty, offers them a cigarette and they accept. Of the two, one looks about twenty-five, the other more like forty. Just as all prison memoirs always have a good warder, so this round-up had to have its tender-hearted SS. The legend which later grew up around them in the Ghetto would have them be Austrians.

'We take away all Jews...' the older one answers the woman. She slaps the palm of a hand against her cast.

'But me, I broken leg...I go away with family... hospital...'

'*Ja, ja,*' agrees the 'Austrian', and motions for her to scarper. While she waits for her family to show up, it occurs to Signora S. to make the most of her friendship with the two soldiers to see if she can save some of her neighbours. She too calls up from the street:

'Sterina! Sterina!'

'What is it?' the woman answers, as she appears in the window.

'Run for it, they're taking everyone!'

'Just a moment, I'll get the kiddie dressed and come down.'

Unfortunately dressing the kiddie sealed her fate: Signora Sterina was taken with her little boy and the rest of her family.

From Via del Portico di Ottavia come sounds of wailing mixed with shouts. Signora S. peeps out from the corner where Via Sant'Ambrogio joins the Portico. It's all too true they're taking everyone, everyone without exception, worse than you can ever imagine. Down the centre of the road in a straggling line trail the families which have been rounded up: an SS man in front and another bringing up the rear mind each group, keeping them more or less in line and prodding them on with the butts of their sub-machine guns, although no one offers any resistance other than tears, sobs, pleas for mercy, baffled questions. Already on the faces of these Jews and in their bearing, more marked even than their suffering, resignation is imprinted. It almost seems this sudden appalling shock already no longer astounds them. Something within them recalls forgotten ancestors who goaded by persecutors such as these trod the same steps towards deportation, enslavement, torture, autos-da-fé. The mothers, some fathers too, carry their little ones in their arms and lead the older children by the hand. The children search their parents' faces for reassurance, comfort they can no longer give; and this is more harrowing even than having to say to one's children 'there's nothing' when they beg for bread. Even so, it's only a matter of time: if they're not killed before, the moment for that too will come. Some kiss their children: a kiss they try to conceal from the Germans, one last kiss here among these streets and houses which witnessed their birth and the first time they smiled on life. Certain fathers rest a hand on the head of their child, the very same gesture with which on holy days they used to impart the *Birchàd Choaním*—'May the Lord God bless and protect you...' —that prayer which both invokes and promises peace for the children of Israel.

Among those in the line Signora S. sees Zia Chele, an eighty-year-old halfwit: she is struggling along among the others, almost skipping, with no notion of what she is being made to do, waving to onlookers and flashing inane and even somewhat frivolous smiles; but then she suddenly starts and takes fright, mouthing snatches of prayers, when the Germans begin shouting again. They shout for no apparent reason, probably only to keep up the terror and reinforce the awe of their authority so as to keep things running smoothly and get the job over with quickly. Another old woman of eighty-five goes by, deaf and sick. A paralytic too, carried bodily in his chair. A woman with a baby at her neck unfastens her blouse and takes out her breast, squeezing it to show a soldier she has no more milk for the child, but he presses his sub-machine gun into her side to keep her moving. Another woman grabs a German's hand and kisses it in tears to stir his pity, implore God knows what minimal favour, or perhaps merely because she is grateful, from the depths of her humiliation, he did not treat her more brutally. She is answered with a punch and a bellow. Motionless, speechless, and powerless to come to their aid, bystanders look on from both sides of the street; but then suddenly the Germans have had enough of these spectators and with threats start gesturing to them to disperse.

A young man leaves the line: his SS escort, who then declines to 'keep him company', has granted him permission to take a coffee. He swallows noisily, the little cup quivering in his hands, with his legs dancing under him too. His dazed eyes turn to the little tables where he used to sit playing cards in the evenings which still had a tomorrow. With a kind of timid, tired smile he asks the café owner:

'What will they do with us?'

These meagre words are among the very few that they left us as they went away. They permit us to hear the voice of a being who for a moment returned to this life of ours, who though alive in our midst no longer had any role in it, having already entered upon that bleak and terrible new existence. And they tell us also what passed through the heads of these hapless people in the first moments: a forlorn hope they had not fully understood.

The columns were driven towards the ungainly little building which houses the Antiquities and Fine Arts offices and stands at the bend in the Portico di Ottavia, opposite Via Catalana, between the church of Sant'Angelo and the Teatro Marcello. Close beside the building is a small archaeological area cluttered with ruins, several metres below street level. The Jews were herded into this pit and lined up to wait for the three or four trucks shuttling between the Ghetto and the location established for the first step of their journey. These lorries were roofed in dark tarpaulin (it continued to drizzle) which some insist had actually been painted black, as they similarly claim of the trucks themselves. It is more probable this black was visible only to eyes of grief and horror, for in reality it must have been the dark and already dismal enough muddy lead colour paint which is the standard uniform, so to speak, of all German military vehicles. True, the Nazis adore orchestrating spectacle, lugubrious and horrifying Nibelungen rites; but here spectacle was already inherent in things themselves, and anyhow superfluous, for everything proceeded according to plan, with no need to propitiate success with any particular stage effects.

The trucks' right sideboard would be lowered and loading would begin. The sick, the handicapped, the reluctant, were spurred on with insults, yells, shoves, and blows from rifle butts. The paralytic on his chair was literally flung into the truck, like an unserviceable stick of furniture into a removals van. As for the children, they were torn from their mothers' arms and treated like packages when postmen are loading up. And then the trucks set off again to no one knew where; though their regular reappearance, and always the same ones, implied it could not be very far distant. And this may have kindled some sort of hope among those rounded up. We're not being sent out of Rome, they're keeping us here for work.

The comb-out lasted until about 1 p.m. When it was over there was not a soul to be seen in the streets of the Ghetto, desolation reigned as in Jeremiah's Jerusalem: *How doth the city sit solitary that was full of people...* All Rome was appalled. In other parts of the city, the round-up followed the same procedure as in the Ghetto, though naturally in more dispersed fashion. The city had been divided into a number of sectors: to each was assigned a lorry which called successively at every doorway marked on the list. In the early hours of the morning when they were found still locked, the SS had them opened up by Italian police. Generally an NCO remained behind to guard the lorry while two soldiers went into the house. If the apartment looked middle-class or reasonably well-off, the first thing the soldiers did was to demand the whereabouts of the telephone and rip the wires out. There is a story that a worker in Prati, spotting the NCO on guard was momentarily distracted, jumped into the cab and drove off at top speed with all on board who beyond their wildest expectations suddenly found themselves freed. (Personally, however, we have not come across a single one of these people so miraculously saved.)

The SS conducting the comb-out belonged to a specialized unit which had arrived from the north the previous evening, without the knowledge of the many other German troops stationed in Rome. Some of these young men could scarcely believe their luck at having the free run of a vehicle, even if packed with captive Jews, to do some sightseeing while in the city. So before being delivered to the collection point, the poor wretches in the back had to put up with the most demented peregrinations, more and more perplexed as to their fate, and at every new turn and every new street assailed by fresh conjectures, all of them alarming. Naturally the chief attraction for these tourists was St Peter's Square, where several trucks remained standing for some time. While the Germans rehearsed many a *wunderbar* with which to stud the account they dreamed of sharing with some Lili Marlene back in the fatherland, from inside the vehicles arose shouts and supplications to the Pope to intervene, to come to their rescue. Then the trucks set off again, and that last hope vanished too.

The Jews were massed together in the Army College. The trucks drove straight in and pulled up by the far colonnade. Offloading proceeded in the same savage and summary fashion as loading. New arrivals were made to line up in threes at a certain distance from similar groups already marshalled under the watchful eye of numerous German guards armed to the teeth. Between one group and another a few Italian fascists were seen circulating with the disdainful air of inspectors and the smug satisfaction of the well-heeled on a day out.

After a certain point they were formed up in squads, and when the women had been separated from the men all were herded into the college lecture halls. Here a limbo-like penumbra prevailed since the shutters had all been tightly sealed. From outside in the yard—where all day chaos reigned—could be heard the plaintive cries of distress mingled with gasps for air emanating from those rooms. Every so often a menacing order bellowed in Italian re-established a momentary and possibly even more anguished silence. A few hours in those packed rooms were all it took to generate that foul odour of stagnating life which presides like a miasma over all prisons and places of deportation. Guards and sentries almost always refused access to the toilets. The intent to humiliate and demoralize these people and reduce them to remnants of humans with no will of their own and no longer almost any self-respect, was immediately apparent.

Very possibly the Germans had not dreamed of such a complete success. The numbers rounded up exceeded all predictions, at least judging by the premises earmarked to hold them, which very quickly proved inadequate. A great many people who could no longer be accommodated in the lecture halls had to be left out under the colonnade. The men in best shape, those whom it was feared might 'try something', were made to stand with their faces to the wall in the by now classic position, both humiliating and intimidating, devised by the Nazis as far back as their earliest persecutions of the Jews. If children tried playing together the sentries made the mothers stop them, with the usual threat of instant execution. A few pallets were spread on the ground and the order was given to lie down on them.

During the night two women went into labour. In both cases the Italian doctors diagnosed difficult births which would need operating. Hospitalization for these women would have been the route to freedom. But the Germans would not consent to their transfer, so the two infants first opened their eyes in the darkness under that hapless colonnade. What names can possibly have been given to these two firstborn of a new Babylonian captivity? (Gershom, 'a stranger in a strange land', was the name Moses gave to his son by Zipporah born in bondage, but the two born that night without Moses were little strangers destined for the gas chambers.)

A boy suffering from a suppurating abscess was instead granted permission to be attended to in hospital. But

Germans were present at the operation and reclaimed the lad the moment it was over.

So they passed the Saturday night, and all of Sunday and the Sunday night. In the city and in the Ghetto meanwhile word had spread about where the unfortunates had been taken to. Their relatives, claiming to be 'Aryan' friends, arrived at the college gates and handed in provisions and notes for the captives, though they never discovered whether this small solace ever reached its destination.

Towards dawn on the Monday the detainees were put into closed lorries and taken to Roma Tiburtina station where they were packed into cattle trucks which then stood idle on a siding for all the rest of the morning. A score of armed Germans barred anyone from approaching the train.

At half-past one the locomotive was entrusted to engine driver Quirino Zazza. Almost at once he realized that in the cattle trucks 'were indiscriminately confined'—as a report by him states—'numerous civilians irrespective of sex or age, whom I later ascertained to be of Jewish race'.

The train moved off at two. A young woman on her way from Milan to join relatives in Rome recounts that at Fara Sabina (but more probably at Orte) she came across the 'sealed train' from which issued voices as of souls in Purgatory. Through the grating on one of the wagons she was almost sure she recognized the face of a little girl, a relative of hers. She tried calling out her name but another face came to the grating and gestured to her to stop. This entreaty for silence, not to attempt to recoup them for mankind, is the last word, the last sign of life to reach us from them.

In the vicinity of Orte the train found a signal against it and had to halt for some ten minutes. 'At the request of the passengers inside'—the driver's words again—some trucks were opened up so that 'those in need might alight to perform their bodily functions'. There were several attempts at escape, promptly quelled with abundant gunfire.

At Chiusi there was another brief stop to offload the corpse of an elderly lady who had died during the journey. Engine driver Zazza came off duty at Florence, without having managed to speak to any of those he had taken on the first stage of their journey towards deportation. After this change of personnel, the train proceeded for Bologna.

Neither the Vatican nor the Red Cross nor Switzerland, nor any other neutral state has managed to obtain news of the deportees. It is estimated that those alone rounded up on 16 October amount to more than a thousand, although this figure is certainly too low since many families were abducted in their entirety without leaving word of themselves, nor a single relative or friend in a position to report their disappearance.

November 1944

Samia

Sandro Onofri

It was night and I was tired and likely that's why at first I couldn't make out what was that smudge of white the same tone as the columns in the side of the bridge. It was all some time ago, I can't say I remember precisely how things went, not now. I should think it was midnight or one in the morning, I don't know, I'd had a killing day, never out of the car. It had just stopped raining, possibly it was still spotting a bit. I remember the lights changed to green, I drove on over Ponte Marconi, but not until I was right across did I realize the white smudge glimpsed moments before out of the corner of my eye wasn't one of the parapet columns but a shirt. And it was not on this side, the pavement side, as would be the case with lingering lovers or some pensioner blissfully filling his lungs with his last cigarette of the day while gazing at the river. No, I was convinced of it now: the shirt was on the other side of the parapet, suspended over the Tiber right beneath, sluggish as pap, churning in its fatty flow a mix of water, clouds, and night. I pulled the car over and walked back to check whether I might still have been mistaken, but after only a few steps I soon realized unfortunately that was not the case. There was the shirt, hanging over the void, and by now I could also distinguish two long sleeves stretching back to clutch the railing. As for the rest, I could just make out the outline of the head, as though stuck onto the neck, gazing downward transfixed.

I rang the 113 emergency on my mobile, with frantic deference letting the operator take me through all the routine questions to check it was not a hoax, then I positioned myself in a corner to wait. Because frankly I had no idea what to do. If I approached the figure suspended over the river, how was I to know whether I wouldn't hasten his decision? On the other hand, there he was still, staring paralysed at the darkness beneath. He was frightened, thank God. I could detect, in some way sense, his trembling. So he was wavering, of that I was now certain. A couple of kids on a scooter with a disabled silencer came burbling by, but then abruptly pulled up and came over to where I was standing. They were tittering, from apprehension. And they asked softly: What's that guy up to? Is he going to jump? And how should I know? Stop here, don't go any closer. The police are coming. They know how to handle this kind of situation, maybe they'll have the fire brigade with them.

Then everything happened at once. The kids, probably fed up with waiting, got back on their scooter and took off just as the police car rounded the corner from behind the nearby block of flats, naturally with siren blaring. Instantly it set off in pursuit of the pair who terrified out of their wits skidded and spilled across the road. I had to sprint back to the other end of the bridge to convince the two cops the kids had nothing to do with it. But just as I was struggling to rescue the two unfortunates from an undeserved duffing up, I noticed the white shirt had climbed back over the parapet and in order not to attract attention was making off at a leisurely pace in the opposite direction, before slipping between the cars parked in the middle of the dividing strip on Viale Marconi. Only at this point did I realize he was a young African, a Somali or Ethiopian, eye whites shining bright as lamps. But I said nothing, pretended I hadn't seen him. Having saved my two quaking companions from the fury of their overhasty contemporaries in uniform, I got back into the car and set off in the direction in which I had seen the would-be suicide disappear. I didn't have to drive around for long, soon enough I found him sitting on the edge of the pavement not far from the darkened booths of a street market, head propped on his raised knees. I got out of the car and went and sat down beside him. He didn't even look up. I patted his shoulder and offered him a cigarette. That was a near thing, I said. He took the cigarette. His hand was trembling, no doubt in part because of the cold, for it was already the middle of the night by now and all he had to protect him was that white shirt. But far more from fear, which was still inside him, and shook him right through.

He was no more than twenty, at most twenty-one. There were just us two and the deep stillness of that hour of the night. I don't know how long we remained sitting there on the kerb, side by side, doing nothing but smoke. He was the one to break the ice. He said he was called Feisal and that he came from Mogadishu, that he'd fled from the war, that his father had died two years ago on account of the war and his own stinginess. If it hadn't been for his mania for emptying the tank of his car for fear thieves would nab the petrol my father would still be alive, he said. And right now he'd be with my mother in San'a, or we'd all of us still be in Somalia, now the war situation is calmer. Me, my dad, my mum, and my sister Samia. Then he told me the story of that particular night, how his father Mohammed had gone out to do his bit in the neighbourhood patrol during curfew, and he'd stopped a bullet out of nowhere right in front of their house, just as he was about to let himself in after coming off his shift. If there'd been a drop of petrol in the tank they'd have made it to the hospital in half an hour. Instead they'd wasted three hours trying to find another car with enough fuel in it, then another three to get hold of the doctor who was to operate on him. Meantime Feisal watched his father draining away before his eyes, it was unbelievable how much blood a man can contain. After six hours he was still alive, and he was still alive when he went into the operating theatre, though nearing the end, with his veins all dried up by then. He died under the scalpel, and a week later Feisal, his mother, and his little sister Samia were already on the lorry that in twenty days of following a dirt road through the bush was to take them to Bosaso, where the boat for the Yemen was waiting for them.

I should work, I should study, but I just can't seem to do it. My sister Samia is here with me. My mother stayed back in San'a with relatives. But I wanted to come away, because my uncle was always ordering me about, wanting me to do the work he decided, go to the school he wanted. Once he even slapped me around, and I can't stand anyone laying a finger on me. My father couldn't take it either. I'm like him. So then I agreed to come here to Italy. After we'd been six months in the Yemen, an application for adoption arrived for Samia and me. They were people we already knew from earlier, friends of my father, and my mother turned to them. They seemed good people. And they are, too. But they can't stand our religion, they take Samia with them to church every Sunday. They won't let me observe Ramadan, they say here in Italy there's the church and we have to respect it. I have to read the Qur'an on the sly. They sent me to school, but I can't cope with studying. My head wanders off, I can't see the sense in it, time never goes fast enough. I've tried working. In Somalia I worked too, in a factory and labouring. But here, I don't know why, I don't have the strength, my legs give out, my arms are soft. I can't seem to do anything properly, and I can't stand it when people tell me so. I lost another job tonight, in this restaurant where I was a waiter. The boss was right, I messed up everything, but when he started screaming in my face I couldn't take anymore, I just turned round and walked out. I didn't even take my jacket. I left it there, with all my money. So then I thought I couldn't go back home. They'd warn Samia off following my example, and they'd be right. That's what they've done other times, they're trying to keep the two of us apart. She's young still, she's lovable. They only put up with me for her sake, I know. But I don't want to lose my sister, I'm responsible for her. I promised my mother.

What could I say to him? I trotted out some truisms. I told him depression is a luxury for Italians with loads of money, that he couldn't afford it. I said he had to work for himself and his sister, and graft at it twice as hard in this country because he wasn't Italian and he wasn't white. There's no way round it, that's how things are, I said to him. Then I said the right to commit suicide cannot be taken away from anyone, but that often it can be made to look completely futile by someone who is a real friend, someone assuredly more important than those people who were so good and such turds who were his guardians. But there was no convincing him. I almost had to lift him bodily to his feet, to give him a lift home. I left him my phone number, but he never called. For weeks I checked the local news pages of the papers with trepidation, afraid of reading he'd jumped into the Tiber, this time success-fully. But luckily I never came across anything. I don't know where he is now. Perhaps he is back with his mother, in San'a, or perhaps not, maybe he's still here. I hope he has found the strength to put up with things as they are, I hope for his sake he has been able to find that strange urge to live which takes hold when we no longer expect anything. A kind of grace. I hope it for his sake, and for little Samia.

Exmatriates

Igiaba Scego

In Rome people always run, in Mogadishu no one ever runs. I come halfway between Rome and Mogadishu: I walk at a good pace. You might think I'm running but I'm still walking. When my mother decided to leave Mogadishu for a better life here in Rome that was the first thing that struck her about the Romans, their constant running about. Just the thought of the women's calf muscles horrified her: 'Oh my God, poor things! Their ankles must be thick as aubergines. It's just not refined.' For Mum refinement is fundamental. Not for nothing are her idols Coco Chanel, Jacqueline Kennedy Onassis, and a certain Howa Harago, a person known only to her, who in Mogadishu and environs was all the rage for her ladylike ways. I could see her so well then, my mum, revolted by the crudity of the world. I can see her so well now: shaking her head, wrinkling her nose in disgust, and then a disapproving silence followed by that slow and inexorable bobbing of the head.

That's why I was so terrified that particular afternoon. Not for anything in the world did I want to see that slow and inexorable bobbing of the head. I would have crumbled— and who wouldn't? The reason for my trepidation was serious. Dead serious. Terrifyingly serious. That afternoon I was going to have to announce to her and everyone else that by the end of the year I intended moving into a place of my own, and bought with my own hard-earned pennies.

Inconceivable! Inadmissable! Unladylike!

What's more, I was going to bring along a certain person who most definitely would never pass unnoticed. For the first time in years I'd be introducing someone new to Mum, and not just to Mum. And on top of that it had been spelled out to me: 'Unless strictly necessary, please don't pollute us with strangers.' Which left not many categories of people palatable enough to bring along to an afternoon tea based on whipped cream. It's true I knew no end of people: dim and slim, fat and freaky, dyed and daft. Some a bit stoned, some decidedly out of their skulls. But nobody suitable for Mum's afternoon tea based on whipped cream. But then, bingo, Angélique. One hundred per cent whipped cream. Besides, between you and me

I was in need of moral support, no way was I going to be able to see it through all on my own.

Attending that show-trial-by-another-name afternoon tea would be the entire clan at 3, Via Gori, staircase B, flat 15. The entire clan being my aunt Sofia, my cousins Zeinab and Mulki, Sofia's daughters, and my little brother Omar. Not to mention, need I add, my own dear materfamilias, Nura Mohamed Jama, of the Sacad tribe, renowned in our neck of the woods as implacably bloodthirsty torturers, slaughterers, assassins, and heaps more cheery things which would make the eponymous hero of the *Exorcist* die with laughter. I don't know how bloodthirsty Mum is, I've not yet seen her clutching a Kalashnikov. But she sure is implacable. So I already had a good mental picture of how she'd massacre Angélique. She'd make mincemeat of her, and then like as not have her for breakfast along with that acidulous brew of coffee, ginger, and unidentified substances with which she's wont to start the day.

From all I've said it must sound like I almost hate my mother. Instead I love her. Adore her. Worship her. Revere her. Take my hat off to her. Which doesn't stop me being scared of her too at times. And that afternoon was one of those times.

The problem, as I knew well, was not the colour of Angélique's skin. To Mum and the rest of the clan it would make not a hoot of difference if I dragged along a white friend or a yellow. And it was not the problem of religion I agonized over. Hare Krishna, Protestant, Jew, atheist . . . all such matters are minor details to us. No, mine was a problem that all the movies of Hollywood or Cinecittà in all their long history have never tackled. Not even Woody Allen, not even that notorious crackpot has ever touched on my kind of problem. And Woody, so far as paranoia and other weird stuff goes, is practically world champion. I was all on my own in this. I had the sole rights. Some bargain! Couldn't I have had sole rights to something better? French kisses with suction effect, say, or Californian prunes. Instead I had sole rights to that one shitty problem. I'd discussed it with my girlfriends, and not one of them had ever gone, 'Oh, me too'. I was well and truly alone in this one.

Alone. Alone. Totally alone.

My problem, guys, was suitcases.

Suitcases, cross my heart. Those parallelepipidons in which we stuff our gear when we have to go somewhere, usually faraway. Call them bags or haversacks or just plain luggage but they're all the same in essence: parallelipipidons or some such geometric shape. In Japan they've even come up with hexagonal ones, the stuff of intergalactic travel. I saw it in a late-night documentary on Rai 3. The fact is in Italy anything odd or curious or interesting only ever gets shown in the middle of the night. In prime time all you get is a grand proliferation of tits and bums, inanities, pretty tarts, ageing presenters, young men with perfect artificial suntans, siliconed transsexuals, lots of belly and not much cellulite, and ratings, ratings, ratings . . . and zilch humour. But then there's this late-night universe with cutting-edge reportage, subtitled Bergman films, genuine political satire. One night I even came across a documentary with gnus, that sort of cow with a beard which used to brighten up so many of my childhood afternoons but which is now a threatened species in the TV schedules. It's the truth, late at night you can find just about anything, even an Italy which no longer exists, even a gnu which no longer exists. And I just happened to hit on that stratospheric suitcase. Out of this world! Oh, out of this world! Zip fasteners more or less all over, pockets more or less all over, the weirdest things more or less all over. And then that ultramodern design, so space age. I've always said the Japanese are streets ahead of everyone, specially where the superfluous is concerned.

Yes, I wouldn't have minded that Japanese suitcase . . .

That one only, though. The rest of the suitcase family was rubbish as far as I was concerned. Goddamned suitcases, they were nothing but torment, agony, and misery for me.

I've good cause to hate them. They've invaded my life for as long as I can remember. We had them on an industrial scale at home, so many we'd have put the best luggage dealer in this city to shame, and in all shapes and colours. Mulki, just the week before, had bought herself a psychedelic one in fuchsia velvet. Mulki, see, is mad about trashy pop and so she absolutely had to have a pretty whacky case in which to store the cream of her huge CD collection, which runs the full alphabetical gamut from Abba to ZZ-Top. Sooner or later, I know it in my bones, ZZ-Top will also invade what little physical space is left to me in this house. Or have they already done so and I don't even know it? That darn ZZ-Top! Anyhow I've never liked them, they scream too much for my liking. I'm more into soft jazz, I'm more the Herbie Hancock type, if you know what I mean. But with all those CDs of hers Mulki was going way over the top, she drove me spare. Too many suitcases and too many discs. At least if she'd had just one Herbie Hancock ... Hell no. Besides, recently she'd been veering towards heavy metal ... always listening to certain horrendous stuff, poor us!

But Mulki wasn't the only one to go over the top.

Oh dear me no, not the only one.

The fact is every member of the family had his or her own suitcases, and quite naturally stored their entire existence in them. Their clothes for starters, but then of course everyone has their own eccentricities too, in which case a suitcase may reveal a universe.

For instance Auntie Sofia, Mulki's mum, possessed a beautiful suitcase bought in Lisbon from when she immigrated there. Its metal handle and pastel shade of chestnut soothed the spirit of whoever set eyes on that marvel of nature. At times I couldn't get my head round the fact that that wondrous object was a mere miserable suitcase. The leather was in a league of its own, after all these years it still smelled good and genuine. Auntie Sofia, who is a great devotee of Allah and his Prophet (peace be upon him) had decided to dedicate that marvel to the things of God. So she'd filled it with all God's things: rosaries, various editions of the Qur'an in various languages, tapes of obscure Egyptian imams, the songs of Yusuf Islam—better known by his Western name of Cat Stevens—and a cream dress which she kept jealously stored away against the day she would make the pilgrimage to Mecca, as every good Muslim must do at least once in a lifetime, funds permitting. Even Omar, my little monster of a brother, who had just hit eleven, had a suitcase all to himself. There he secreted his thoughts, his colouring books from when he was little, the plastic models of his favourite footballers (he had a good fifty identical ones of his hero Francesco Totti), his toys, and the love letter he'd written to one of his little schoolmates with a blue streak in her hair which he'd never had the guts to post. Each of us had a mass of suitcases. Not least the materfamilias. She had no less than five and was proud of all five of them. Four were for clothes and other bits and bobs, the fifth was a total mystery. In all these years—thirty, come March, I regret to say—she had never once let me near that mysterious suitcase. Of course I was dying to see what was inside! I'd have given anything.

Naturally I too had my own suitcases. But I hated them. I mistreated them. I changed them frequently. The fact is those suitcases drove me insane. What I'd have liked was a good strong wardrobe. I'd have liked to keep my things in less of a mess. I'd have liked security.

Instead in my home the word wardrobe was taboo. As, for that matter, was the word home, the word security, the word roots, the word stability.

All abstract concepts to my family. Illogical!

But the truth is all those suitcases hid our anxiety, our fear.

Mum would always say, 'If we keep everything in suitcases, when the time comes we won't need to pack in a great big rush.' 'When the time comes' indicated some vague moment in the future when we'd make our triumphant return to Mama Africa's bosom. In other words: grab those suitcases, board that plane, grand homecoming in our Sunday best, happiness sublime, heat, and tropical fruit.

Our problem lay right there, in that puerile, infantile dream.

In our hearts the dream had a name, a secret name we never uttered. We didn't want to spoil it, or worse.

And so we waited . . .

And we waited . . .

And waited . . .

And then nothing. The moment never came! We were in perpetual wait for a return to the mother country which in all likelihood would never happen. Our name for our living nightmare was *dismatria*. At times someone would correct us and say: 'No, in Italian we say *espatrio*, the state of expatriation, of being far from your *patria*, your fatherland, just as you are all expatriates, *espatriati*.' We would shake our heads, give a disparaging sneer, and with no compunction say it again: *dismatria*. We're exmatriates, not expatriates. Someone had severed—perhaps for ever—the umbilical cord attaching us to our *matria,* our mother country of Somalia. And orphans, what do they normally do? Dream. And that's what we did. We lived on that dream, that waiting, much like the Jews live in wait for the Messiah. Neither we nor the Jews are sure it will ever happen, and perhaps that doesn't matter too much, sometimes it's enough just to have the dream. And so that's how we lived, pretending to be jovial, cheerful, carefree, just like other people. In our hearts, though, we bore the torment of the exiled. In our heart of hearts we knew we would never again go back to Somalia, to our Somalia, because the fact was our Somalia no longer existed. But rather than admit this simple truth we preferred to pull the wool over each other's eyes. Somalia, the dreamed-of, the longed-for, the endlessly desired, lived on solely in our daydreams, in the chatter of women at night, in the smells of food on feast days, in the exotic scents in our hair. Even I and Mulki, who had barely set foot in Somalia, fed off that pain. And little Omar too, who to all intents and purposes had never seen Somalia, every once in a while shed a little innocent tear for that land he had never got to know. In truth, the civil war (but how can a war ever be civil?) had put paid to the dream of return. Of course we could go and see the Somalia of today, that monstrous assemblage of warlords, corruption, and hunger. Of course we could! We could even decide to live there. We only had to catch a plane from Dubai and fly off to what was now a no-man's-land where the governments of the rich world had elected to dump their toxic waste. But it wouldn't have been the same, as I knew full well, and so did all the rest. Our Somalia was dead, defunct, over and done with long ago. But we, like everyone else who chooses to ignore the evidence, pretended that She, that capricious woman who tormented us, had only absented herself a moment to powder that pointy nose of hers which distinguished her from her African sisters. So that's why we had no end of suitcases, that's why we didn't buy wardrobes, that's why the word home was taboo. Security, stability, settling down, becoming Italian...it would all have broken our beautiful dream. We were kidding ourselves and each other, and sadly we were all only too aware of it.

But as for myself, I'd had enough! I was fed up! I was pissed off! I wanted a wardrobe, no matter how small. A home, no matter how small. A life, no matter how short.

Oh God, you who see everything, all I wanted was stupid reality. My own stupid reality.

That's why I adored furniture stores. It was not rare for me to be sighted outside one of these establishments lost in contemplation of various manifestations of solidly functional wood wardrobes. I was in love with wardrobes. Spellbound, infatuated, seduced, head-over-heels. There were times I even longed to be a good solid wardrobe myself. Oh, if I believed in reincarnation (pity I don't) I'd beg Buddha, Shiva, or whoever else: 'Please, in the next life let me be reborn as a wardrobe.'

A wardrobe is one of the most classic elements in the furnishings of a house. People persist in seeing it as an encumbrance, but I see it as a light shining in darkness. But people, as we all know, often just don't get even the simplest thing about life. How often have I heard someone say: 'Oh, my wardrobe's so in the way', even 'It takes up so much space', and 'I can't breathe' is another favourite. But the most ungrateful and definitely worst thing is: 'I wish it would disappear'. Next thing they're trying to sink it into the wall, even worse banish it to some dark recess far out of sight, in so-called dressing rooms. When this can't be done (not everyone has surplus square feet to squander) some sort of 'sensible' arrangement has to be found which also takes into account the position of the bed in relation to the window. So then the brain gets busy and starts to ponder: 'Where the fuck can it go?' And in no time imagination runs riot and comes up with a bizarre and far-fetched *pas de deux* of possibilities. Alongside, opposite, above, below, at an angle, at a slant. 'So darling, what would you say to a wardrobe with sliding doors?' Often the 'darling' in question is not in agreement with the 'darling' who questions. But in my experience of wardrobes there is one thing I've understood: women go for sliding doors, men being more traditionalist love to hear the clash of separate doors, perhaps it reminds them of their mother's breast.

And from there it's but a step to wardrobes becoming battlegrounds for the historic and never-ending war between the sexes. We row over wardrobes, grab each other by the hair, even divorce. And why? Because when all is said and done we human beings don't understand the profoundly simple philosophy of this noble and austere item of furniture. I don't doubt Socrates and Plato would have appreciated it so much better. But were there wardrobes in Socrates' day?

Anyhow, I'm for the free-standing type, and specific-ally what is known here as the 'island' variety, that is to say your wardrobe set plumb in the middle of the room, your Wardrobe King. It wouldn't be in the way, I'm certain.

No way would it be in the way. So now THREE CHEERS for the ISLAND, my very own ISLAND!

That afternoon, though, there was no talk of ward-robes, in fact I believe at the start there was no talk at all. The eyes of the entire clan were riveted on the person of Angélique. Eyes swarming with question marks. All tacitly posing questions. And some seemed to be coming up with answers. I did nothing to contradict their suppositions. But neither did I endorse them.

Every one of them was a born newshound, gossipmon-ger, insatiable seeker after the sensational. And all the same they held their tongues, nobody wanted to be the first to jump the gun. Consequently, apart from busying themselves with preparations, no one did a thing.

Angélique's presence had totally thrown them. That was the first time they'd seen a drag queen so up close. When I got to know her, Angélique still called herself Angel. And he was nothing like the stereotypical homo-sexual, he didn't mince, he wasn't monstrously vain, he didn't wiggle his hips. He walked straight and true, in perfect harmony with his body weight.

I'll never forget the day I got to know him, five years ago. I was working in a shop and he'd only just arrived in Italy from Brazil. He looked me over, then asked in his own language: '*Fica aberta toda noite?*', with that last word pronounced 'noy-she', Pelé-style, heavily accentuated on the last syllable. All he wanted to know was whether the place stayed open all night. But I gave him a massive clout which almost took his right ear off. I thought he was after a one-night stand, and what's more took me for a whore, *fica* being 'cunt' in Italian. I almost died of shame when someone finally explained to me it just means 'stay' in Brazilian and nothing like what I thought. But the slap made us good friends, and still today Angélique talks of that slap as a kind of miracle because thanks to this anecdote she pulls loads of men, and then also 'because that's how I got to know *você minha querida*'—darling you.

So, partly out of friendship and partly because she owes it to me that she pulls so many blokes, she agreed for my sake to put her head on the block for that afternoon farce with my family.

Auntie Sofia was staring at her tits. And Mulki and Zainab were staring at her tits.

They sure were big tits. Drag queens are as spectacular as firework displays in this matter.

Mum, though, was simply watching. She was the only one to realize Angélique wasn't there to scandalize or as a provocation. Something else was afoot. That's why she was simply watching me and not Angélique.

I hate being watched. With Mum I always feel I'm under a sodding great microscope.

'Nothing escapes my tribe,' she always used to say, and it's just a pity my needs and desires escaped her. Oh God, would I ever be able to tell her about the flat?

I surveyed the table. I calmed down a bit. My little family had pulled out all the stops that afternoon. The table was groaning with good things. With every delight known to East and West. It looked like a cross between Christmas dinner and the evening meal that breaks the fast during the holy month of Ramadan. Every inch of the table was taken up. Three sorts of herbal tea, two kinds of coffee, one flavoured, one not. Fruit juice galore, various sweets, various salads, various pickles. A feast for the eyes. And Zainab had made her great speciality too: having lived for years in Egypt she had prepared a meat and chickpea stew, something guaranteed to make you hear angels carolling. A shame, though, that no one took the initiative to start the banquet. We were lost in contemplation, and no one could bring themselves to go into action. Clearly, everyone was waiting for Angélique to make the first move.

Of all of us, she was the calmest. In fact she was the only one not totally absorbed. While I quaked in all my being she even managed to smile. She had lovely teeth and loved to display them. She was not at all vain but was justly proud of her perfect set of teeth. Not one crooked tooth, no fillings, no caps, no bothers. This spared her the humiliation of the dentist's chair every year, and a lot of cash. Angélique was not specially beautiful, perhaps she wasn't even pretty. But she had class, she was refined. And this had not escaped the materfamilias's eagle eye. Mama Nura aspired to everything that was in the least refined. And this even outweighed her prejudices against 'perverts' (as she chose to term them). And this is why she flashed three great big encouraging smiles in the direction of my drag friend.

Minutes passed and nothing happened.

Then Angélique, visibly bored by the general silence, finally started to ogle the spread on the table. The rest did too, but covered it up well. She, being no cover-upper, stared more and more avidly at the table. She spotted something succulent to the north-east of a thermos full of one of the three herbal teas. She slowly turned her head to the west, but with her hand still aiming straight for that succulent and tempting east. To be the first to dive in at a buffet requires greater discretion, spontaneity, and humanity than any other art. You're guilty of gross violation, but then no one will remember you when it comes to the trial. We're all guilty in the end.

The hand shot out and Angélique's jaws went straight into action. The east had been assailed. Angélique had relished the booty. Her palate revelled in the meat packed inside that little fold of puff pastry. It wanted a second shot at that little fortress of savouries. Everyone else, envious of the outsider's success, followed suit.

It was all over very quickly. I hardly noticed it. I don't remember now, but I too surely must have partaken in that orgy of edibles. All the anguish I felt hadn't killed my appetite.

I surveyed the table that had been so neat and orderly. A tornado had torn through it. Every inch of the table had been plundered. The three sorts of tea had been drained, the two kinds of coffee gulped down, the fruit juices sucked up. And what can I say about the various sweets, the various salads, and the various pickles? Destroyed in the maelstrom of various jaws in action. Chewed, enjoyed, digested. Zainab's stew had been among the first to vanish into various intestines. In short, the food had done itself proud. Only that in all that bedlam of chatter and munching one crucial sound had been missing: the sound of the voice (and jaws) of my mum. She had not uttered a word and had not tasted a thing. She had confined herself to sipping a traditional coffee with no sugar. In other words, the city had been conquered but not the citadel . . . only then could victory be declared.

Mum was watching me again. Examining, investigating, scrutinizing me with her left eye, while her right eye bored into my soul.

I looked back at the materfamilias. I wondered when she would explode. And I wondered whether I'd ever find the courage to tell her what was eating my heart.

I looked at Angélique, and perhaps I begged for help.

Mum stared at me once more for a very long time. Sipping what was left of the coffee in her cup.

Then she moved next to Angélique, shoving me out of the way. I'd thought I was the one she was going to address, after all that examining and investigating. Instead she addressed the drag queen and said: 'What are you doing here? You're nothing to do with us. You're not one of the family. And, Signora, I don't know whether you've noticed, but you're a pervert, in a word a homosexual.'

She said that word 'homosexual' with a quaint detachment.

Maybe this was my moment at last. I had to speak, I could feel it so strongly. Speak up in Angélique's defence, and my own. Explain. Explain that I could have (in fact had) friends who were gay. That I had a life outside those four walls and that my life outside was free of suitcases. And that I'd soon be leaving. That I was going to buy a flat. And that I would put a wardrobe in it. And that I felt

Italian. And that feeling Italian didn't have to mean betraying Somalia.

Only I just couldn't manage to get out a single word.

Angélique, who is my angel, stepped in for me. And all she said was: 'Thank you for bringing it to my notice, I've had a vague suspicion since I was thirteen. I used to imitate Maria Bethânia in front of the big mirror in my parent's bedroom. Do you know Maria Bethânia?'

Mum had been wrong-footed.

'No. Should I?'

'Not necessarily. But . . .'

'I know Maria Bethânia!' cried Mulki in the mumbling fashion of someone with their mouth full (evidently she'd laid in a little stock of cakes). With these words she got up and left the room. She came back with a suitcase, not the fuchsia suitcase but a poo-coloured one.

'If I open it will you tell me where you got your tits done?'

'In Morocco, baby, in Casablanca.'

'Morocco . . .' echoed the girl, scarcely able to believe those stratospheric tits came from the country that manufactured more emigrants than anywhere else in the world. She didn't wait to be asked, not Mulki. With great ceremony she opened up the poo-coloured suitcase and extracted a disc with on its cover a Masai woman extending a hand towards the infinite.

Angélique didn't even look at the Maria Bethânia disc. She went straight over to Mulki's suitcase. She caressed it like a boyfriend's body and then to our total surprise brutally tipped out its contents. The discs lay all over the floor like corpses. World-famous names, truly world-famous, lay scattered all about like the fallen of the Great War: David Bowie, the Bee Gees, John Denver, Simon and Garfunkel, the Beatles, and of course them too, the infamous ZZ Top. The discs lay inert. Pathetic. Lifeless. Mulki wept. 'Why?' she cried. 'Why?' she snivelled.

'Because it's ridiculous!'

'What?' chorus all the women.

'To keep your stuff in suitcases, not living, castrating yourselves. It's absurd! But can't you see it's absurd? You marvel at my tits, you think I'm crazy, but you're the ones who are crazy... don't you realize?'

Then she did something even more astounding. She grabbed me violently by an arm and thrust me right in front of my mother.

'Speak to her!' she ordered.

Everyone waited for me to speak. I was a coward and couldn't bear to speak, be confrontational, let them all down.

I looked at the discs on the floor. I saw a Bill Evans amongst them too.

And then I understood, I understood everything. It was clear what I had to do and so I did it. I spoke.

'I want to buy my own flat, Mum. I want to go and live on my own. I want a wardrobe too, and no more suitcases, never again.'

Mum aged thirty years before my eyes. No one in the family had ever spoken to her like that. I had broken the exmatriates pact. I was a rebel pariah.

'But you can rent, my girl, find a place to rent, you don't have to buy a flat, this isn't our country.'

'No, Mum . . . I have to buy it. Rent is money thrown away. I want something that's mine at the end of the day. I want a little place of my own in this world—and then, Mum, this is my country.'

I hugged her like I'd never done in all the thirty years we'd known each other, and the years fell away from her again.

I felt the warmth of her in my arms, and for the first time I felt her small and frail.

We were exmatriates, orphans, all alone in the world. We needed to give ourselves hope, fuck it. Our embrace lasted to infinity. Then, when infinity finished, we discovered ruins all around us. Everyone had emptied out their suitcases. And lo and behold our sitting room had filled up with things both familiar and never seen before. Hair grips, hair pieces in all colours of the rainbow, floral bracelets, books of poetry, black-and-white photos, ancient evening bags, colour magazines, discoloured scarves, cotton shawls, yellowing postcards, chipped rosaries, worn down eyeliners, old VHS films, used batteries, rag dolls, cracked incense burners, empty picture frames, dented transistors, work scissors, unopened floppy discs, pristine notebooks, and many, many too many things more. Our clothes, our secrets, our torments. All out there on the cold bare floor. I too ran off to empty my suitcases. And strangely so did Mum. She emptied out all four. Not the fifth.

'You do it, my girl,' she said.

And I did it. I opened up her case as a treasure trove deserves to be opened, as Tutankhamen-obsessed Howard Carter at last opened up that tomb. I opened it and at first I saw nothing. Only a fusty acrid smell of staleness assailed my nostrils. Then I began to make out things. The weirdest things. A packet of spaghetti, photos of historic monuments in Rome, a cat's fur, a plastic Parmesan cheese, a tacky souvenir of the she-wolf suckling the twins, some earth in a bag, a little bottle filled with water, a stone... and so many weird things more. I looked at Mum and so did everyone else. One question mark in all our eyes.

'What's it about?' asked our eyes.

'I didn't want to forget Rome,' said Mum with a sigh. And then she smiled.

We all looked at each other. Big smiles all round. We hadn't known it, but we had another *matria*.

Romulus and Remus

Alberto Moravia

The pangs of hunger are like nothing else. Try saying out loud: 'I need a pair of shoes... I need a comb... I need a handkerchief', and stop for a moment to draw breath, then say: 'I need a meal', and straight off you'll feel the difference. Anything else you can have a good long think about, look around, take your pick, maybe even drop the idea, but the moment you confess to yourself what you need is a meal, there's no time to waste. You have to find that meal or die of hunger.

On 5 October this year, at noon in Piazza Colonna, I sat down on the railing by the fountain and said to myself: 'I need a meal'. I'd been staring at the ground when I had the thought and when I looked up again the traffic on the Corso had gone all foggy and trembling: I hadn't eaten for more than twenty-four hours and, as is well known, the first thing to happen when you're hungry is things around you start looking starved too, that is all feeble and tottering as if it's everything else but you that's famished. Then I thought I had to get me this meal, and I thought if I wait any longer I'll not even have the strength to think about it, and I started pondering the quickest way to get it. Sadly, when you've no time left you don't think too brilliantly. The first ideas which leapt to mind weren't ideas but dreams: 'I get on a tram . . . nick this guy's wallet . . . run for my life,' or: 'I walk into a shop, head straight for the till, grab the swag . . . run for my life.' I started to nearly panic and thought: 'Seeing I'm done for anyway, I might as well get myself arrested for insulting an officer of the law . . . the fuzz are bound to give me at least a bowl of soup.' At that moment a lad beside me called out to another: 'Romolo!' Well now, at that shout I remembered another Romolo who had been a conscript along with me. Back then, I just somehow couldn't resist telling him a pack of lies: that I was considered pretty well off in my home town, for instance, whereas in fact I first saw the light of day just outside Rome, at Prima Porta. Still, right now that little porky could save my bacon. Romolo had opened a trattoria in the neighbourhood of the Pantheon.

I'd go there for the meal I needed. Then, when it came to the bill, I'd start on about our old friendship, comrades-in-arms, all the memories . . . In short, Romolo wasn't ever going to get me arrested.

The first thing I did was to go up to a shop window and look at myself in a mirror. By good luck I'd had a shave that morning, procuring razor and soap from the landlord, an usher at the law courts who rents me this poky little room under the stairs. My shirt might not have been overly clean but it was decent enough, this was only day four. My suit, grey twill, was good as new, I'd got it off this kind-hearted widow of my captain from the war. My tie, though, was pretty frayed, the same red tie I'd had for ten years. I turned up my collar and redid the knot, though that made one end too short and the other far too long. I tucked the short end behind the long and buttoned my jacket all the way up. When I turned away from the mirror, possibly because I'd been concentrating so hard on my appearance, my head was spinning and I bumped right into a cop standing on the corner of the pavement. 'Watch where you go,' he said, 'you drunk or what?' 'Yes, drunk with hunger,' I should have answered. With tottering steps I headed in the direction of the Pantheon.

I knew the address, but when I got there I couldn't believe my eyes. It was a little door at the end of a blind alley right next to four or five overflowing dustbins. The oxblood-coloured sign proclaimed home cooking: *Trattoria, cucina casalinga*. The window, in the same red, contained nothing but an apple. One apple, no joking. I was starting to get the picture, but having come this far I walked straight in. Once inside, it was even more plain what the situation was and for a moment my hunger intensified my dismay. But I took my courage in both hands and went and sat down at one of the four or five tables in the darkened and deserted little room.

A filthy hanging behind the counter concealed a doorway leading to the kitchen. I thumped my fist on the table: 'Waiter!' Straight off there came sounds of movement in the kitchen, the hanging shifted, and a face which I recognized as belonging to my old mate Romolo appeared and disappeared. I waited a while longer, then thumped the table again. This time he came rushing out hastily buttoning up a battered white jacket all spotted with grease. He approached me with an ingratiating 'At your service', all brimming with hope which made my heart fair bleed for him. But by this time it was in for a penny in for pound. I said: 'I want something to eat.' He started going over the table top with a rag, then stopped and stared: 'But you're Remo...'

'Ah, now you recognize me,' I said, smiling.

'Why of course I recognize you...we were in the Army together. Didn't they call us Romulus and Remus and the She-Wolf on account of that girl we were both chasing after?' So there you go: wheel out the memories. I could tell he was harping on the good old times not out of any fondness for me but because I was a customer. Or rather, seeing there was no one else in the entire place, *the* customer. He couldn't have had too many and so the memories were as good as anything else to make me feel welcome.

At the finish he clapped me on the shoulder: 'Good old Remo', then turned towards the kitchen and called out: 'Loreta!' The hanging was pulled aside to reveal a stout little apron-clad woman with a grumpy and suspicious look on her face. Motioning to me he said: 'This is the very Remo I've told you so much about.' She gave me a wan smile and lifted a hand in greeting, while behind her peeped out their children, a boy and a little girl. Romolo went on: 'Good fellow...good fellow'. Since he kept par-roting 'Good fellow' it was obvious he was waiting for me to start ordering. I said: 'Romolo, I'm just passing through Rome. I'm a commercial traveller now and...seeing I needed to eat somewhere I thought to myself: "Why not go and eat at my old pal Romolo's?" '

'Good fellow,' he said. 'Now what can we do for you really special—spaghetti?'

'Perfect.'

'Spaghetti with butter and Parmesan...that way you won't have to wait so long and it's lighter on the stomach...After that what do you fancy? A steak? Couple of slices of veal? Nice little bit of sirloin? A veal cutlet done in butter?'

They were all simple things, I could have cooked them myself on a primus stove. I said, cruelly: 'Roast lamb. Is there roast lamb?'

'Sorry, no...we're doing it for tonight.'

'All right then...Just a fillet steak, with a fried egg on top—à la Bismarck.'

'À la Bismarck, sure...With potatoes?'

'Salad.'

'Right, with salad...And a litre of white. Dry, eh?'

'Dry.'

Chanting 'Dry, dry' to himself he went off into the kitchen leaving me alone at the table. My head was still spinning I felt so faint, and I realized only too well I was totally out of order, but I couldn't help feeling just a little bit pleased with myself. Hunger makes you cruel. Romolo was probably even hungrier than I was, and at bottom I was glad of the fact. Meanwhile, out in the kitchen the family was confabulating together. I could hear him speaking in a low voice, urgent and anxious, and his wife answering him moodily. Finally, the hanging parted and the two kids dashed through and shot out the door. I realized Romolo very likely didn't even have a crumb of bread in his trattoria. When the hanging shifted I'd caught a glimpse of his wife on her feet at the stove fanning the dying embers. Next he too came out of the kitchen and sat down opposite me at the table.

He had come to keep me company so as to distract me until the kids got back with the purchases. Again out of cruelty I asked him: 'You've got yourself a nice little place here... So how's it doing?'

He answered, with his head down: 'All right, not bad... Of course these are tough times for everyone... Then today's a Monday... But most times it's bedlam in here.'

'So you're well set up, eh?'

He looked at me before replying. He had the round fat face of a restaurateur, but pale and distraught and with several days' beard. He said: 'You're well set up too.'

I replied offhandedly: 'Can't complain... I can generally reckon on making a hundred, a hundred and fifty thousand a month... It's a hard life, mind.'

'Not half as much as ours.'

'Yeah, maybe... You restaurant people are in clover, everyone can manage without most things but they still have to eat... I bet you've got a fair bit stashed away.'

This time he said nothing, just smiled: a pained smile which made me feel a little bit sorry for him. In the end he said, almost imploringly: 'Good old Remo...remember when we were in Gaeta?' In other words, he was clutching at memories because he was too ashamed to lie, and maybe also because that had been the best time of his life. This time my heart really did go out to him, so I contented him by conceding I did remember. At once he perked up and started talking again, slapping me on the back once in a while and even laughing. The boy came back clutching in both hands, on tiptoe as though it was the Holy Grail, a litre carafe full to the brim. Romolo filled my glass and then his own as soon as I urged him to. With the wine he grew even more loquacious, a sure sign he was starving too. So what with the chat and the drink another twenty or so minutes went by, and then as if in a dream I saw the little girl coming back. Poor thing, her thin little arms were hugging a bundle holding a bit of everything: the yellow package containing the steak, the egg in newspaper, the baguette in flimsy brown paper, the butter and the cheese in greaseproof, the green bunch of salad, and, as far as I could make out, even a bottle of oil. She went straight into the kitchen, all so serious and pleased with herself, and as she passed behind Romolo he shifted in his chair to hide her from view. Then he poured himself another and started in on old memories again. Meantime,

out in the kitchen I could hear the mother saying something or other to her daughter, and the girl apologizing
and saying very softly: 'He wouldn't give me any less.' In
short, sheer unadulterated poverty, just possibly even
worse than my own.

But I was famished, and when the girl brought in the
plate of spaghetti I lashed into it with no regrets; in fact
the feeling I was scrounging a meal off people as down on
their luck as myself gave me an even bigger appetite.
Romolo enviously watched me eating and I couldn't
help thinking that just like me he wouldn't be treating
himself to a plateful like that too often. 'Try some,'
I proposed. He shook his head as though he wanted to
refuse, but I scooped up a good forkful and shoved it in
his mouth. He said: 'Nice, I will say,' as though talking to
himself.

After the spaghetti the girl brought me the fillet with
the egg on top and the salad, and Romolo, ashamed of
sitting there counting my every mouthful, returned to the
kitchen. Ah, what a treat it is to eat when you're hungry!
I popped a piece of bread in my mouth, moistened it with
a sip of wine, chewed, and swallowed. It was years since I'd
eaten anything with such relish.

The girl brought in the fruit, and I asked for a bit of
Parmesan to go with the pear. When I'd eaten my fill
I leaned back in my chair chewing a toothpick, and the

whole family came out of the kitchen and stood in a circle before me, eyeing me like a rare animal. Probably because he'd had a bit to drink, Romolo was merry now and deep into some tale about one of our escapades with women when we were in uniform together. His wife, though, her sweaty face smudged with charcoal, was anything but happy. I looked at the kids: they were so pale and under-fed, with eyes almost as big as their heads. I suddenly felt a real pang of pity and remorse. Even more when the wife said, 'Ah, we could do with four or five customers like you every mealtime . . . then we'd be able to breathe.'

'Why?' I asked, all innocent, 'Don't people come?'

'A few, yes,' she said, 'but more towards the evening . . . Just poor people. They bring their own bite to eat, order some wine, not much, a quarter litre, maybe a half . . . Mornings I don't even light the fire, because nobody ever comes.'

I don't know why these words had such an effect on Romolo. He said: 'Hey, cut out all the moaning . . . you'll bring me bad luck.'

His wife snapped back: 'You're the one who brings the bad luck. You're the jinx round here! Here am I slaving away worrying myself sick and you do nothing but spend your time reminiscing about when you were a soldier, so who's the jinx?'

They were going at each other like this while I, half befuddled because I was feeling so good, was mulling over how best to get out of the little matter of the bill to pay. Then, by good luck, Romolo suddenly flew off the handle: he raised his hand and slapped his wife across the face. She didn't hang about. She ran to the kitchen and came straight back out with a long sharp knife, one of those for slicing ham. Screaming 'I'll kill you!' she ran at him with the knife aloft. Terrified, he scuttled away from her round the room sending tables and chairs flying. The girl burst into tears, the boy dived into the kitchen too and came out waving a rolling pin, I still don't know whether to protect his mother or his father. I realized this was my moment or never. I got to my feet saying: 'Calm down, for God's sake calm down,' and still mumbling 'Calm down, calm down' found myself in the alleyway outside the trattoria. I sprinted off, nipped round the corner, slowed to walking pace in Piazza del Pantheon, and headed on back to the Corso.

The Small Hours

Corrado Alvaro

With each new season word flies round Rome of some undiscovered place to eat. It's one of the few novelties of the year. For a while, post-discovery, the regulars who come for the wine and bring their own lunch pack are still granted their old haunt just inside the door, along with the counter, the barrels or flagons of wine, the cold snacks, the salamis. Beyond, in the converted back room still dank from all the long drab years of poverty, the new customers who will make the establishment's fortune take their seats. Next, the locals' front-of-shop is dispensed with to extend the little dining area, but still the girls in the family serve table with almost maternal devotion, the solicitude of providers of food for the famished. Later, a chic clientele with a nose for such novelties packs the place advertising its presence by turning the street outside into a parking lot; and now the family grows less expansive, the daughters no longer wait at table, more often than not the landlord's sudden prosperity makes him morose and tetchy. Meantime the advance guard of discoverers has long decamped for pastures new.

I have belonged to one of these bands of friends since the days when I had certain artistic aspirations which eventually I had to shelve in order to apply myself to a more remunerative profession, in civil engineering. Still, I like to keep up with the old crowd, frequent the same set of long ago. I remember there was a time when we used to make plans for bettering so many things in our lives and cherished hopes that would better the lives of everyone. That doesn't happen now. Seemingly now it's enough simply to comprehend, agree on the ways of the world, as though everything carries on in some other realm of no relevance to us. All we know is life in Rome begins in November and ends in May; everyone seems well-off and happy while the sun shines; the odd week of rain looks like sheer spite; then there'll be some new film, a couple of plays, more tittle-tattle in the papers featuring mostly women and young girls, some new lass whose photos make her look as scintillating as a freshly caught fish.

One evening early last summer, not long after we discovered the Osteria della Sibilla in Trastevere, we were eating outside on the little piazza where the 'Rome by Night' coaches make their last stop and linger a while. That night—the weather was warming—a few bored passengers sat listening to the elucidations of their guide who then got down to stretch his legs leaving his charges on board in the middle of the dimly lit square right opposite the osteria, all lost in thought inside that shiny machine smelling faintly of its own components, the inescapable odour of modern-day travel. I was picturing to myself how the spectacle of the little square, the osteria, the people eating at tables, would imprint itself on the minds of these strangers and long after resurface in memory far from here. All at once, on one of those impulses with which Italians attempt to dispel the first hint of something sad, from our table Orazio began waving wildly at that coach marooned in the quiet of the night, and we followed suit, waving as though we had just caught sight of old friends far beyond reach. The tourists roused themselves, unsure how to react at first, until energized by our same irrational enthusiasm they eventually began to return our greeting. We watched them drive off, heads turned back, hands still fluttering, as though on the very point of departure they had discovered the warm heart of a foreign city they had struggled hopelessly to comprehend, the mystery of an impenetrable existence opening up just as it has to be abandoned. We too seemed to feel our spirits soar at that instant, for we harboured the same longings and delusions we had helped to rouse.

We have always stuck together, more or less the same group all these years, and almost all of us have done well for ourselves. Orazio, a young architect back then, has even struck rich, with some big firms on his books, and yet he has unfailingly kept faith with the old band. He comes from the Po Valley and has not lost those sudden bursts of enthusiasm typical of his people, so that Rome's inertia or indifference still gets under his skin. His wife is a much later addition to our company but she has taken easily to our ways, and she is wholly enchanted by some of her husband's whims. The fact is that Adriana, as she is called, comes from a family of artists and she had the very special education you acquire in families of that sort, rather like among the good old-fashioned country nobility. It's a certain way of conducting oneself that would not be out of place at some minor princely court which one often finds in artists' offspring, a distillation of experience, empathy, and no doubt a tinge of world-weariness. Adriana studied ballet as a girl and at times the passion for dance possesses her again, much as we others too can be seized by a sudden wild urge prompted by some magic hour in Rome, a yearning to achieve something momentous, and all it is is the nocturnal spell of this city, when the pointless bustle of the day recedes and you feel there is still time for everything.

The emotions of that scene with the coach had excited us all; doubtless we'd also had a bit to drink. We drove off through the narrow lanes of Trastevere, all of us, eight or nine people in three cars. I happened to be in the first, next to Orazio who was driving. In the darkness the district seemed sunk in a sort of sleepy reminiscence of life as a village, with its rustic-looking houses, and the rubbish, and the cats—when from one of those lanes we spotted three figures approaching, plainly foreigners: two men and a woman, not speaking and very probably lost. The street was narrow, they pressed their backs against the wall. As he levelled Orazio pulled up and stuck his head out to say with that barely concealed excitement I knew signalled one of his sudden inspirations: 'Where are you going? Come with us. Get in, there's room!' The three of them exchanged glances. I saw the woman in their midst, stupefied, platinum hair and two intense black eyes in the pallor of her face. Orazio looked back and shouted at the car behind: 'You with all the space, let them in.' The trio climbed aboard. As Orazio drove off we demanded: 'Who are they?' He shrugged. 'Don't ask me. Three bored foreigners, I don't doubt.' Adriana said nothing. I knew so well her way of falling silent awhile, lost in admiration of her husband's capacity to create an occasion, engineer the unexpected. As for Orazio, he looked delighted with himself, like a hunter bringing home a prize trophy.

At the Swiss bar, still packed at that hour, where Orazio stopped to buy provisions for the evening including several bottles of whisky, we had our first good sight of the foreigners. They had all got out with us and stood watching us make our purchases without the slightest reaction. We presumed they were English. We felt like actors in a somewhat reckless production. Everything was proceeding without introductions on either side, and here we were possessed by this absurd idea of putting on a show for people who knew absolutely nothing about us, or we of them, and with sole responsibility for the success of the evening. It was one of those situations in which Orazio revelled, with his curiosity about his fellow man, the unknown human being, and his gift of connecting with others. Even after all these years he was incapable of resigning himself to the loneliness of Rome, this life without meaningful connection, nothing but the mutual irritation of an overcrowded city. He was constantly going out of his way to endeavour to exchange a word with someone, communicate for no cause and without sounding off, simply in order to feel human among humans. While taken up with his purchases, it struck me the three foreigners were eyeing him as though at any moment some action of his would betray the real meaning, the actual purpose of this event in which they partook like explorers. As he exchanged a few phrases with these unknown people I started observing him through their eyes, as a person bent on staging an evening from which he must surely expect something in return, unless he was laying some unfathomable trap. And the three of them, meanwhile, looked resolved to embark with good grace on this adventure in an unknown land about which strange legends circulate. Orazio's outlay was totally disproportionate to the situation. Our guests eyed him quizzically, wondering where it would lead: at any event they would have their good Italian story to tell.

It seemed to me that in Orazio's studio, where we went to spend the rest of the evening, there unfolded one of those scenes one reads about in the accounts of travellers in Italy a century ago, when they report how in a world steeped in memories of an irretrievable past now seemingly peopled only by wan custodians, themselves victims of some unspecified form of alienation, they actually happened to meet up with some quite remarkable folk who still preserved a spark of the ancient genius, masters of an art which at the very least is still the art of living. Our guests were in no time at their ease, for as soon as they appeared to discern in us who knows what long-lost attributes they began reminiscing about things equally remote, journeys and encounters, as though relaying tales of curious creatures in the forest, and this forest was the world. The older man, the lady's husband, had got to know people in many countries, and certain names that turn up in the newspapers began to assume, in his stories, physical shape, an ordinary everyday life of their own. The night grew vast, stretched right to the furthest ends of the earth, and in the most far-flung cities, in a single room, appeared people alive like us, who like us longed to hear of the lives of equally remote people with tenuous names capable of evoking a compelling presence. Later, Adriana treated us to one of her dances. There arose, like the thoughts that come in the small hours, a nocturnal Adriana, clad in a pair of tight green corduroy trousers and a black blouse. It was two in the morning.

The evening was over. Rome was plunged in that brief hour of silence in which she recovers her arcane significance, her stillness and majesty in which there is time for everything, freed from her inconclusive daytime delirium, the rush to get to the office and fritter away the day. The three of them took their leave. It had been an evening with no discernible purpose, and when the door closed behind them we asked each other: 'Do you think they had a good time?' We were never to discover any more about them, or they of us.

It was Adriana, some other evening, who recounted the aftermath of that encounter. 'You know those

foreigners, they got in touch later. Next day, from one of
the biggest hotels in Rome I got a call from the lady who
never said a word all evening. She told me she and her
husband and his friend had rarely enjoyed themselves so
much with anyone else in their entire lives, it would be so
nice for everyone to meet up again, and they invited us all
for dinner with them the following evening. I don't know
whether I did the right thing. I told her we were all leaving
for a long trip together that very day, and were so sorry
not to be able to accept. I couldn't help remembering how
that evening had been a happy and successful invention
during which we all found each other agreeable, interesting, intriguing. Perhaps meeting up in a hotel dining
room we'd have found each other unremarkable, possibly
insufferable. There are so very few things that happen
for no reason, unscheduled, unpremeditated. We should
respect them.'

The Sound of Woodworm

Giosuè Calaciura

His ears bother him. A constant rustling. Wings, wings of the angel who has quit his stony pose on the bridge under the Castle and come fluttering sleepy-eyed right into his room to announce the dawn. Another day dawns, Holy Father, a miracle.

Twenty-five years, like perpetual insomnia. Twenty-five years confounding him and consoling him. He suffers from solitude. Like God. Holiness, how do you feel?

I feel like the lambs that come into this world only to have their throats slit at Easter, I feel transparent, right through, like stigmata, I feel like Jesus in the Garden of Gethsemane. I feel old.

The angel preens his feathers just like the mournful gulls of the Tiber, opens the window and flies back to his stone perch on the bridge.

Twenty-five years of somnambulant nights watching the miraculous play of shadow and light on the ceiling. Daybreak. He crooks his elbows, settles a steadying foot on the floor, pushes down with all his might, and is reborn. Like Lazarus. With infinite care he shuts the window left wide open by the thoughtless angel, and contemplates the miracle.

Every night he confuses the sound of the woodworm eating St Peter's with the Chamberlain's stealthy tread. Tiptoeing upstairs to check he breathes. The Holy Father breathes.

But it is not the woodworm, and not even the Chamberlain. It's the creaking of the Mystery.

He is certain of it. They want to ease him out of power. Without a rumpus. The ageing process. So at breakfast, to spite them, he calls for papers and accounts, checks revenues and outgoings, how much this parish spends and how much that, and how much it makes up for in charitable donations, and how many pilgrims per coach, and how many Swiss guards, and the archbishops, the seminarians—and do we want the Christmas crib again this year? The shepherds, the sheep, the manger halfwit, the fisherman, the empty crib, the baby Jesus? And the Wise Men? Three as usual, or does someone want to muscle in?

His little game. They obey without demur. Because they all have a guilty conscience. Every morning at breakfast, with their account books and their lists of souls.

All a charade. These twenty-five years. He's certain of it.

To get him out of the way they stick him on a plane every so often and post him round the world to explain God. Non-existent journeys.

He's certain of it. Implacable as the will of God they whisk him away, speeding through the city on the VIP lanes, out to the airport where once upon a time the ancient Romans fancied they could fly. They winch him aboard in a harness and announce take-off. A farce. In actual fact he spends days on end in the cockpit of a bomber left over from some American war, shot down and abandoned halfway home because it was pointless taking it right back across the Atlantic. Reconditioned as papal aeroplane. No engines, just a cocktail of sound effects to dupe him. He's certain. To simulate bumpy weather the Apostolic Nunzio behind him jogs his seat. And so just to humour them all he blesses the thunderclaps and lightning flashes produced by the Cinecittà resistors applied to the windows. Thus does the Almighty manifest Himself. He comforts the sick and the terrified, they weep tears dispensed from eye-droppers, and he goes from seat to seat reciting a rosary: Each one of us is alone before God, with our doubts, with our hands which tremble, and he slips the pilot a knowing wink. He sights cherubim among the cloud scenery, flitting alongside to indicate the route. They don't fool him. They are cardboard angels of the Lord from the parish musical props department of the Don Bosco Theatre for the little orphaned children's Easter play. He pretends not to see. He knows they haven't taken off. And after days and days of this claustrophobic quarantine they announce the plane is landing. Before negotiating the steps he winks again and exclaims, Oh how big the Good Lord's world has grown.

He's certain. And while they make him play the tourist they have the time of their lives tinkering with the divine correspondence at the bidding of new associates who have their own way of fiddling the Church's affairs.

They make him get down onto this improbable patch of South America devoid of Christians. And once again he reads from the communiqué they put in his hands: We are all called to be disciples. He looks about him and cannot hide his distress that the world is now the same everywhere. He senses it in the squalor of the airports, the stench of carrion drifting from continent to continent, and the look in the eyes of these camouflaged campesinos identical to the ground staff at Fiumicino. And the duplicity of it all he finds still more unbearable when they compel him to kiss the ground of this corner of God's Creation that has supposedly never seen a Christian, while instead he's been put out of the popemobile on the edge of some dilapidated outskirt abandoned to the solitude of goats so that no one will spot the old dupe descending from his vehicle with the slowness of millennia.

They'd built him the mobile altar to prevent him straying off to bless all and sundry when the springtime crowds gather. Last time he crossed St Peter's Square on his tottering toddler's legs he'd forsaken the red carpet routes, and to the horror of the ranks of cardinals and of the Swiss Guards rolling their eyes at the *carabinieri* to implore them to stop the old chap, he had discovered a gap along the barrier, terrifying the faithful who had not expected His Holiness to make a detour and suddenly found him close enough to smell the papal breath, the whiff of old flesh from Poland garnished with a superfluity of incense rising from a wheezing fagged-out pope whose shuffling steps scattered all before them, so close they could even hear the tormenting night noise in his ears. Yet no one was slow enough to stop him. And so he ploughed onward, blessing *urbi et orbi* to right and to left, to open a breach and make his way through, creating havoc in the square. So intense was the proximity of salvation that the most impressionable fainted into the arms of their carers from shock at what looked like the commotion surrounding a miracle, and no one was sure if what they were seeing were paralytics who had risen from the confinement of their wheelchairs or the blind who no longer sensing a friendly guiding arm were wandering about in obedience to their inner light. And so he blessed to left and he blessed to right, indiscriminately and with no concern for rank, stumbling at times and grabbing onto the nearest person, baring to St Peter's sunlight the sores of the terminally ill at the last gasping hope of their journey, the secret tumours of adolescents, the incurable pangs of the sick at heart, and then somehow suddenly he was far beyond the colonnade where the mollycoddling laws of the Holy See no longer apply and where instead the rule of scoundrels flourishes and the arrogance of godless punks on scooters who insult him, rubbing up against him like serpents. Out of me road, grandad.

The angels of security, ears buzzing with orders direct from God, reclaimed him and settled him back inside the popemobile, and to prevent further escapes pulled the safety belts extra tight. With encouraging pinches they compelled him to greet the crowds. And the faithful watched him blessing as though he was imploring their help.

They delivered him safely back to the solitude of his somnambulant nights, the patrolling Chamberlain, and the irritation in his ears like the swishing of wings.

The angel who announces dawn came back. Together they listened to the sound of the woodworm eating St Peter's till the creatures were gorged and fell silent at last. Then they flew away, escorted by Tiber gulls, the few miles down to the sea. And seeing by now the sun was high continued on their way.

Notes on the Authors

1. **Giovanni Boccaccio** (1313–75), Tuscan humanist, scholar, poet, and consummate storyteller, left a great many influential works in both Italian and Latin, but is now remembered chiefly for his immortal *Decameron*, a collection of one hundred tales in Italian ranging from the tragic to the ribald, recounted by ten young Florentine fugitives from the Black Death of 1348. As readers of Dante will know, the materialism and corruption of the Church hierarchy was evident to all, and gave rise to several popular movements for a more spiritual life, most notably that of the Franciscans.

2. **Pier Paolo Pasolini** (1922–75), poet and film-maker and the most challenging polemicist of post-war Italy, was born in rural northeast Italy but moved to Rome in 1949. His early fiction and cinema explore the lives and language of youths living on the margin of society in the capital. The present story, very much in this vein, was written in 1953–4. The penitentiary is Rebibbia prison, to the east of Rome, near which Pasolini was living at the time. Pasolini's poetry and the Roman novels are available in English.

3. **Giacomo Casanova** (1725–98). The 4,000-page unfinished *Histoire de ma vie* was written up from the Venetian adventurer's diaries during his last years in the service of the Duke of Waldstein in order to beguile, as he said, 'the dreadful tedium which is slowly killing me in Bohemia'. The first 'Thérèse', the soprano Angela Calori, had been one of his earliest loves, re-encountered by chance

in Florence in 1760. This was Casanova's second visit to Rome after an absence of fifteen years. Signora Cherufini was Cardinal Albani's mistress.

4. **Erri De Luca** was born in Naples in 1950 and lives in Rome. His many works draw extensively on his Neapolitan background, his passion for mountaineering, and his years of militancy in the Roman section of the radical leftist group *Lotta continua*. His most recent writing is strongly influenced by the experience of teaching himself Hebrew and translating afresh several books of the Old Testament. Available in English: *God's Mountain* (2002) and *Three Horses* (2005).

5. **'Anonymous Roman'.** The so-called 'Life of Cola' (*Vita di Cola*), written in the Roman vernacular, is only one section of the unknown author's chronicle of fourteenth-century Rome, most of which has not survived. One of the Roman 'people', though from the wealthier middle class which had at first backed Cola's anti-baronial revolution, he was clearly witness to many of the events he describes. Mine is an abridged version, condensing Cola's two brief periods of rule into one.

6. **Goffredo Parise** (1929–86) was born in Vicenza but lived much of his restless life in Rome. Poet, novelist, and *Corriere della Sera* special correspondent in the United States, Japan, and the war zones of Vietnam, Parise also published brief prose pieces of hallucinatory intensity, best exemplified by his masterwork *Sillabari* (translated as *Solitudes* in English), from which this story is taken. Another recommended read is his posthumously published novel with a Roman setting, translated as *The Smell of Blood* (2002).

7. **Melania Mazzucco,** one of Italy's most gifted new writers, was born in Rome in 1966. Her latest novel, her sixth, is inspired by the working partnership between the Renaissance painter Tintoretto and his daughter Marietta. Though widely translated elsewhere, the only one of Mazzucco's novels so far available in

English is *Vita* (2005) about her emigrant forebears in America. Her novel *Un giorno perfetto* (2005) was made into a film by Ferzan Ozpetek.

8. **Ennio Flaiano** (1910–72), novelist and screenwriter, was born in Pescara on the Adriatic coast but settled in Rome. The most astute observer of his adopted city among writers of his generation, he co-wrote with Tullio Pinelli all Fellini's films between 1950 and 1965 including *I vitelloni* (1953), *La strada* (1954), *La dolce vita* (1959), and 8 ½ (1963). The text here is an abridged version of the original. Flaiano's non-chronological presentation of his journal reflections is of course deliberate.

9. **Francesco Mandica**, born in Rome in 1974, is a writer-presenter of cultural programmes for Rai 3 (Italian national TV). His poetry and stories have appeared in the Rome-based literary journal *Accattone*, which takes its title from Pasolini's first film.

10. **Elisabetta Rasy,** novelist and literary critic, was born in Rome in 1947. She has published several studies of women's writing, as well as imaginative accounts of the lives of St Teresa and Mary Wollstonecraft. One of her more recent novels, *Tra noi due* (2002), is an evocative story of growing up in Rome in the early 1960s.

11. **Matteo Bandello** (1485–1561), by his own admission no great stylist compared to Boccaccio, was a Piedmontese nobleman, prelate, and courtier with a huge love of gossip and tall stories. His lively *Novelle* comprise 214 tales, among them the originals for Shakespeare's *Romeo and Juliet* and Webster's *The Duchess of Malfi*. Among the several thousand prostitutes who serviced Renaissance Rome, at the top of the profession were the well-rewarded 'courtesans', women particularly favoured by the courtiers and clergy of the Roman curia.

12. **Vincenzo Cerami,** born in Rome in 1940, is the author of several novels and many entertaining slightly surreal short stories set in

Rome. He made his name with *Un borghese piccolo piccolo* (1976), later made into a film starring Alberto Sordi. Cerami is himself a prolific screenwriter who has worked on some forty films, including titles by Pier Paolo Pasolini, Marco Bellocchio, Gianni Amelio, and Roberto Benigni.

13. **Giorgio Vigolo** (1894–1983), as this story makes plain, was born in Rome. He was a poet and music critic, and the author of several other very evocative pieces on his native city. In 1952 Vigolo published the first modern critical edition of the over 2,000 sonnets in Roman vernacular ('romanesco') by Giuseppe Gioachino Belli, 'the great poet of Rome' (see Tale 3).

14. **Dacia Maraini,** novelist, dramatist, poet, children's writer, and leading feminist commentator, was born in Florence in 1936. She spent her girlhood in Sicily and in 1954 moved to Rome where she later lived with Alberto Moravia. More than a dozen of her works exist in English translation, among them *Woman at War* (1989), *The Silent Duchess* (1993), *Voci* (1994), and *Violin* (2000).

15. **Giacomo Debenedetti** (1901–67) was one of Italy's finest literary critics of the last century. Of Italian Jewish parentage, he spent his formative years in anti-fascist circles in Turin. He settled in Rome in 1936 working as screenwriter and film critic, and after the war taught Italian literature at the University of Rome. His account of the Nazi round-up of Rome's Jews was written within months of the event, after he had had to go underground for his own safety: 'I am a critic, this is my only profession. *16 October 1943* was written by one who lived it directly. It is best attributed to a new Anonymous Roman, such as the one who left us the Life of Cola' (see Tale 5). The pages translated here comprise the middle and final sections of the original.

16. **Sandro Onofri** (1955–99), Rome-born author of a fine trilogy of novels set in the capital, was also a dedicated teacher in a marginal secondary school about which he was writing an important book,

sadly curtailed by his early death. His journalism included several memorable pieces about the harsher realities of life in Rome for the left-wing paper *L'Unità*.

17. **Igiaba Scego,** born in Rome in 1974 of parents who fled the 1969 coup in Somalia, works as a freelance journalist in Rome. She has published several short stories and three novels, the most recent (*Oltre Babilonia,* 2008) about issues of dual identity and mother–daughter relations within the Somalian diaspora.

18. **Alberto Moravia** (1907–90) was born in Rome. As a prolific and highly successful novelist and journalist, Moravia was one of Italy's most prominent cultural figures. He was also the author of the original 'Rome Tales', 130 short stories set in Rome, and collected under the titles *Racconti romani* (1954) and *Nuovi racconti romani* (1966). The short stories and all his novels have been translated into English. *The Woman of Rome* (*La Romana,* 1949), his story of a working-class girl's life as a streetwalker, was an international bestseller.

19. **Corrado Alvaro** (1895–1956), born in San Luca, Calabria, was one of Italy's supreme short-story writers. Though he was to settle in Rome, where he worked as a journalist and film writer, the majority of his stories and the best of his longer fiction, such as *Gente in Aspromonte* (1930) translated as *Revolt in Aspromonte* (1962), drew its inspiration from his native Calabria.

20. **Giosuè Calaciura** was born in Palermo in 1960, but for the past ten years has lived in Rome where he works on the Rai 3 TV cultural programme 'Fahrenheit'. His output includes plays for radio, as well as novels and short stories. The story translated here was the germ for his fourth novel, *Urbi et orbi* (2006). The castle mentioned in the tale is of course Castel Sant'Angelo.

Further Reading and Viewing

A few books about Rome

The best English guide to Rome was written by Georgina Masson in 1965. Fortunately it has just been updated by John Fort and reissued under its original title, *The Companion Guide to Rome* (2009). Another very companionable writer on Rome is Christopher Hibbert, who in his well-told and well-illustrated *Rome, the Biography of a City* (Penguin Books, 1985) covers the history of Rome from its prehistoric origins until the 1970s. In *The Secrets of Rome: Love and Death in the Eternal City* (Rizzoli, 2007) the thriller writer Corrado Augias retells superbly many of the most fascinating stories of his city from classical times to the present day. Carlo Levi, the author of *Christ Stopped at Eboli,* celebrated Rome and its people with great affection in a number of articles now collected together under the title *Fleeting Rome* (2005). Pasolini's shorter pieces on Rome appear in *Studies from the City of God: Sketches and*

Chronicles of Rome, 1950–1966 (2003). Look for these and other books on Rome at the Feltrinelli bookshop in Piazza Argentina.

Very little Italian fiction set in Rome has found its way into English. Pasolini's novels of Rome's marginal youth have recently been reissued as *The Ragazzi* (2007) and *A Violent Life* (2007). Moravia's *The Woman of Rome* is now also available again, however his classic *Roman Tales* can only be found second-hand. The two finest works of fiction about Rome, however, are Elsa Morante's *History: A Novel* (1974, reissued 2002 as a Penguin Modern Classic), set in Rome during and after the Second World War, a passionate defence of the struggle of ordinary people against the weight of history; and Carlo Emilio Gadda's quirky thriller *Quer pasticciaccio in Via Merulana* (1957), translated as *That Awful Mess in Via Merulana* (1965), another epic of the ordinary set in Rome under fascism, and a masterpiece of Italian literature.

Cinema

Rome, with Cinecittà at its door from 1937, has been a great centre of cinema production ever since the silent film era. Three great Rome-located films, classics of the so-called Italian neo-realist wave, are Roberto Rossellini's *Rome Open City* (1945), and Vittorio De Sica's *The Bicycle*

Thief (1948) and *Umberto D.* (1951). Before *La dolce vita* (1959), Federico Fellini had already made two superb 'Rome' films: *The White Sheik* (1952), and *The Nights of Cabiria* (1957). An overlooked gem of the same period is Lucchino Visconti's *Bellissima* (1951) starring the great Roman actress Anna Magnani. Fellini returned to the theme of Rome in *Fellini Satyricon* (1969), an extravaganza about the savagery and decadence of imperial Rome, and the brilliant *Roma* (1971), a very personal tribute to the city's fascination for him. Pasolini's first two films, *Accattone* (1961) and *Mamma Roma* (1962), equally personal, were set among those he called the city's 'subproletariat'. A comic classic of this great period of Italian cinema is Mario Monicelli's *I soliti ignoti* (*Big Deal on Madonna Street*, 1958).

Of more recent films there are Nanni Moretti's *Caro diario* (*Dear Diary*, 1993), a witty take on modern Rome, and indeed Italian society in general; Ettore Scola's family saga *La famiglia* (1987), and his *Una giornata particolare* (*A Special Day*, 1997) with Marcello Mastroianni and Sofia Loren, set in fascist Rome, as is also much of Bernardo Bertolucci's superb *The Conformist* (1970). Bertolucci's *Beseiged* (1998) and Agostino Ferrente's *The Orchestra of Piazza Vittorio* (2006) both recognize Rome for the multi-ethnic city it is today. Two fine political films are Marco Bellocchio's *Good Morning Night* (2003) about the period of Red Brigade terrorism, and Paolo Sorrentino's *Il divo* (2009), a dark satire about power and corruption. Michele Placido's *Romanzo criminale* (2005) is a powerful thriller set in Rome.

World Wide Web

Google 'romefile.com' and 'rome.info' for a wealth of information for visitors, the latter with an interactive map of Rome which gives satellite pictures of every location mentioned in *Rome Tales*. Most of the *rioni*, the districts into which by long tradition Rome within the ancient walls is divided, are marked on the map overleaf. Many are mentioned in the tales.

Publisher's Acknowledgements

1. Giovanni Boccaccio, 'Abraam Giudeo', from *Decameron*, i. 2.

2. Pier Paolo Pasolini, 'Dal vero' from *Alì dagli occhi azzurri* in *Romanzi e racconti*, vol. ii. Mondadori, 1998.

3. Giacomo Casanova, *Histoire de ma vie*, vol. vii, ch. 8. Brockhaus, 1962.

4. Erri De Luca, 'La camicia al muro' from *Il contrario di uno*. Feltrinelli, 2005.

5. Anonimo romano, *Cronica*. Adelphi, 1981.

6. Goffredo Parise, 'Libertà' from *Sillabario N.2*. Mondadori, 1982.

7. Melania Mazzucco, 'Autoblu' from *I colori di Roma*, ed. Giuseppe Cerasa. Gruppo editoriale L'Espresso, 2006.

8. Ennio Flaiano, 'Fogli di Via Veneto' from *La solitudine del satiro*. Rizzoli, 1973.

9. Francesco Mandica, 'Lorette Ellerup' from *Roma capoccia*, ed. Lanfranco Caminiti. DeriveApprodi, 2005.

10. Elisabetta Rasy, 'Due giorni a natale' from *Natale con i tuoi*, ed. S. Perella. Guida, 2004.

11. Matteo Bandello, *Novelle*, ii. 51 and iii. 17.

12. Vincenzo Cerami, 'I fratelli caucci' from *La gente*. Einaudi, 1993.

13. Giorgio Vigolo, 'La bella mano' from *Le notti romane*. Bompiani, 1961.

14. Dacia Maraini, 'La ragazza con la treccia' from *La ragazza con la treccia*. Viviani, 1994.

15. Giacomo Debenedetti, '16 ottobre 1943' from *Saggi*. Mondadori, 1999.

16. Sandro Onofri, 'Samia' from *Le magnifiche sorti*. Baldini & Castoldi, 1997.

17. Igiaba Scego, 'Dismatria' from *Le pecore nere*, ed. Flavia Capitani and Emanuele Coen. Laterza, 2009.

18. Alberto Moravia, 'Romolo e Remo' from *Racconti romani*. Bompiani, 1967.

19. Corrado Alvaro, 'Le ore piccole' from *Gente che passa: Racconti dispersi*. Rubbettino, 2007.

20. Giosuè Calaciura, 'Il rumore dei tarli' from *Roma capoccia*, ed. Lanfranco Caminiti. DeriveApprodi, 2005.

Map of Rome

Map showing the *rioni* and some of the sites mentioned in the text.

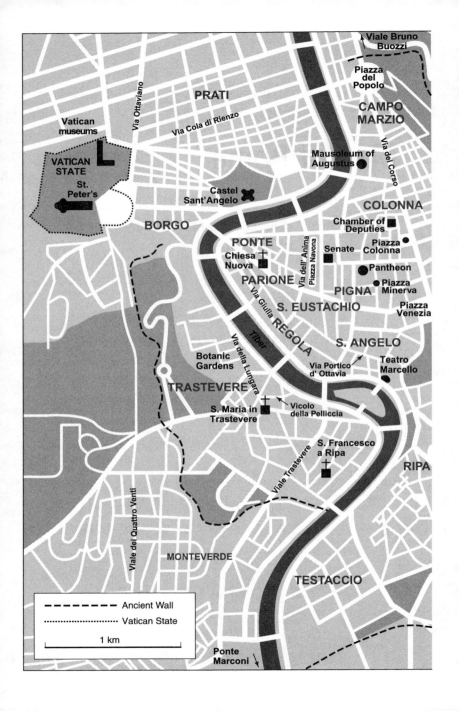

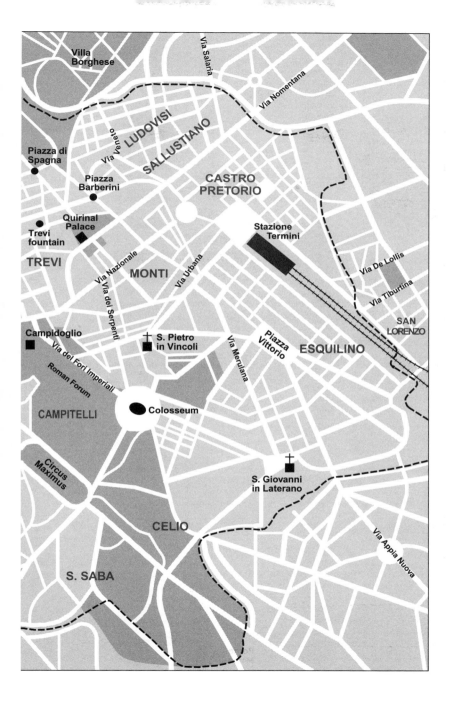